HOUR OF SURRENDER

UNHOLY ANGELS
BOOK 1

KAT LE VEQUE

AUTHOR'S NOTE

They're known as The Unholy Angels.

What a great group of guys this is. I had such a great time writing about them and, in a couple of cases, expanding the stories. Originally, these were separate stories published under different titles, but I really wanted to make this a cohesive group. The guys are all the same age and literally have the same backgrounds, so The Unholy Angels was born—a CIA unit so elite that it's considered the best in the world. The guys in this series, so far—Trace, Reed, and Beau—are considered the best of the best. Hard-core, hard-hitting agents who fight for what they believe in. But then, the twist—these hard-core agents who eventually retire and try to settle back down into civilian life.

That's a tough one.

It's like driving a car 100 MPH for years and then suddenly hitting the brakes and being expected to be okay with that. Being expected to blend in with the normal world around them and assume a normal life. That's the tough part, but the guys do it well and, of course, falling in love is a major part of that.

These stories, however, deal with heavy subjects—assault, murder, racial injustice, and betrayal to name a few. But at the core of the stories is a message: hope. There is always hope. Hope for love, hope for healing, and any number of other 'hopes'. This is a series that introduces a lot of subjects and, hopefully, does it with strength and tact. The bottom line is that these are great guys and I love watching them handle life as it comes at them and eventually fall in love. For good.

Each story in the series starts out with a mission that shows a pivotal moment in the lives of the agents. It explains the stuff they'd dealt with and gives a little background on how they fought—and survived—their job. The heroes definitely have a connection and that continues into their civilian life.

The books in this series can be read in any order:

Hour of Surrender
Hour of Dreams
Hour of Secrets

Just three for now, but there will be more at some point. Until then -

Happy reading!

THE UNHOLY ANGELS

In the Hebrew Bible, a 'destroying angel' is an entity sent by God to dispense His wrath. In the old and new testament, nothing is feared more than the angel of death. In this day and age, nothing is feared more than the specialized CIA unit known as The Unholy Angels.

They come from all walks of life, both military and non-military families. But each man has a military background and training, and each man has decided to go above and beyond for his fellow man. They have become agents, operatives with names like the General, the Intimidator, the Fixer, and more. In the name of justice and freedom, they live by the sword and sometimes die by the sword. It's a world of constant pressure, constant danger, and when an agent transfers out or retires, they often find the real world difficult to live in.

They must find their way.

**Meet the men of The Unholy Angels and the
women who love them.
Loyalty above all.
And a love that outshines the darkness.**

IN THE BEGINNING
EARLY 2000S, MERSIN, TURKIYE

It had been a running gun battle.

They had what they'd come for, but now, in the heat of the late afternoon, those they'd been trying to evade had caught up to them. I didn't matter that they'd changed cars twice to throw them off the scent. That hadn't mattered at all. Through the dirty, dusty streets, avoiding pedestrians and power poles, they'd been fleeing the *Turk Mafyasi*.

The Turkish Mafia.

This was a lesser branch based in Adana, but they had contacts and family members all over the place. Trace, Marcos, Beau, and Reed had found that out the hard way. The op had been simple—extricating a mafia member who had killed a CIA agent and bring him to the ports at Mersin for transfer to a vessel that would take him to a U.S. Navy warship patrolling in the Mediterranean. They'd traced the killer of their friend to his sister's house in Adana and they'd burned down the house and killed about twelve people to get at him.

Now that they had him, they wanted to keep him.

No matter what the *Obalar Mafyasi* had to say about it.

The Obalar family was big in Adana. There had to be a thousand of them, all spread out over the city. A ruthless group that made their money in drugs and weapons and the agent they'd killed had been an undercover operative. A friend of the group of CIA men who were trying to bring his killer to justice.

They were known as The Unholy Angels.

And they were.

Destroyer angels.

"Beau!" Trace Rocklin shouted above the wind that was roaring in through the windows of the Fiat they were in. "You need to either go faster or try to lose these bastards. And watch the flank—they're trying to cut us off!"

Beau Meade, a man born and bred in Mississippi, had a cool way about him. He didn't get worked up about much. But that didn't mean he wasn't on top of what was going on around them.

He knew the stakes.

As soon as Trace shouted at him, he caught sight of a car shooting out at them from an alley up ahead. The car meant to cut them off, but Beau jerked the steering wheel to the left and managed to avoid them enough so that Trace could shoot out their windshield. That sent the car careening into one of the cars that was chasing them and they both went up in flames.

Beau took a hard left and disappeared down another street.

"Are agents meeting us at the port?" he yelled over the wind.

Before anyone could answer him, he had to duck low to dodge a volley of bullets that had just ripped over his head and pinged into the car frame. Trace and the two other men of their group lay down return fire, enough to rupture the tires of the pursuing car that was closest to them.

Beau took another hard right that nearly pitched Trace out onto the street.

"There should be a line of Navy personnel at the port waiting for us," Trace said, gripping the car frame to keep his balance. "Reed? That's your department. We'll have reinforcements—right?"

Reed McCoy, who had come to the CIA after working for the NCIS division, slid into the back seat so he could reload his gun. He was still a Marine to the bone in spite of the fact he hadn't officially been one for years.

"Yeah," he said. On the floorboards below his feet, their prisoner was trying to push himself up and Reed put an enormous cowboy-booted foot on the back of the man's neck to shove him down again. "There should be some Marines ready to reinforce us when we get there."

Trace eyed the big man from Wyoming. "There had better be," he said. "Because we've got Obalar members coming out of our asses. If the Marines aren't there, we're dead."

"They'll be there."

More bullets zinged over their heads. Trace and Reed ducked, but Marcos, who was still returning fire, got winged on the jaw. He threw himself into the back seat, hand over the wound.

"Is it bad?" he asked Trace. "Look at it. Is it bad?"

Marcos was an excellent agent, but he could be excitable. Sissy was more like it. Trace shoved him forward, over the supine prisoner and into the passenger seat next to Beau.

"You'll live," he told him. "Help Beau. If anyone comes around aiming for him, take them out."

Marcos wasn't quite so sure that his good looks weren't forever damaged by the bullet graze, but he didn't say anything. Trace was too hard for his own good sometimes and especially in a crisis, but that's why he was one of the best in the business. The harder the job, the better he performed. The Russians even had a name for him - *istreblyat.*

The Eliminator.

It wasn't as if the others in the Unholy Angels weren't well known to their adversaries, either. There were others in their group, but these men were the core. They had been conducting deep ops for the CIA for about six years as a team and there wasn't one faction, group, or military leader who didn't know their names. Names, in addition to the Eliminator, like *covboy*—or Cowboy as Reed was known.

His adversaries were fascinated by the Marine from Wyoming who was like a real American hero. Beau, on the other hand, was called *komandir* - basically, the Commander or the General. Beau was the brains in situations like this, Trace was the hit man, and Reed was the muscle. Marcos was their communications guru. Adversaries didn't care much about him, but they should have—he was the one who kept the team moving.

Like now.

"There!" Marcos said, pointing off to the left. "The port. See it?"

Beau did. There were cars and shipping containers and buildings between them and the port of Mersin, but he wasn't going to let that get in his way. He drove over a curb, through a pathway, and emerged into the avenue along the beach on the other side. There were people in the way and Marcos hung his head out of the window, screaming for them to get out of the way. They scattered and Beau drove straight through, startling pigeons and seagulls and bottoming out on the curb.

Sparks flew from the under carriage.

More bullets flew overhead, but less than before. Their pursuers had either been lost or otherwise compromised. Or it could have been the fact that there was a dozen or so armed U.S. Marines on the dock, waiting by a small transport vessel to take them to the larger warship out at sea.

"There!" Trace shouted when he saw them. "Go, go, go!"

Beau headed straight for the Marines, who were ready

with their weapons. A few more bullets flew and the Marines returned fire as the Fiat flew off the road, jumped a curb, and hit part of a fence. The fence collapsed, partially on the car, but that didn't stop the men from bailing out of the vehicle and bringing their prisoner with them.

Safety was in sight.

Trace and Reed had the man by the arms, running for the dock and dragging his bound legs along the concrete. There were thousands of shipping containers around them because Mersin was a major port along the Mediterranean. In addition to the cargo ships, there were also several docked ships from the Turkish Navy. In all, it was an exceedingly crowded port and Reed and Trace managed to make it behind the line of Marines, who were covering their retreat along with Beau. He had a wicked-looking Colt M1A4 carbine rifle in his hands and as Reed and Trace ran past him, Beau followed, running backwards to cover them.

"Go, go!" Beau hissed, recognizing one of the cars that had been chasing them as it came around a corner of stacked cargo. "Hurry! Get in the boat!"

Marcos was already in the small landing craft that was docked at the end of a long pier. The pier had other ships lined up against it, so any bullets coming from their pursuers got lost in the steel and iron of the vessels. They had to run at least a quarter of a mile to get from the car to the landing craft, followed by the Marines at this point, and everyone bailed onto the vessel that took off the very second the last man was on board.

Out to sea it went.

The Marines spread out on the boat and they could hear them shouting about being pursued at sea, but the CIA agents were on the floor of the craft, exhausted from their flight. Now that they were at sea, they'd leave it to the Navy to keep them out of the clutches of the Turkish Mafia. On his knees from where he'd leapt onto the boat and dropped his prisoner, Trace had a couple of the Marines take their captive away. As they took the man below, Trace and Reed and Beau managed to get to their feet, watching the port of Mersin fade further and further away. In the wheelhouse, they could hear Marcos on the radio, relaying information about the capture.

Successful.

But, damn...by the skin of their teeth.

"Jesus," Beau grunted, looking for some place to sit down. "I thought we'd never make it."

He found a piece of equipment to perch his ass on and Trace followed him, sitting next to him.

"This is why we get paid the big bucks, boys," Trace said, wiping the sweat off his face. "And tomorrow, we'll do it all again."

"Not me," Beau said, shaking his head wearily. "This is my last one. Reed, too. We're done."

Trace knew that, but he didn't want to hear it. He was hoping they'd forgotten that both Beau and Reed were moving on from the CIA, something they'd both decided last year when a close friend had been killed in the line of fire. These hairy operations were what they did and they were very good at it, but Reed in particular wanted out. He had two young boys he wanted to see grow up, so Trace didn't blame him. Beau, too, was married and the woman spent most of her life alone.

But Trace? He was married. He had a young son. But it wasn't a marriage and he had no family life.

The CIA was his everything.

That was his curse.

"Well," Trace said after a moment. "We've got other guys in our group, but you two...I'm not just losing friends. I feel like I'm losing my brothers."

The boat bounced over the rough sea and they had to hold on or risk being tossed out. When the boat settled down, Beau turned to Trace.

"You're not losing us," he said. "You just won't be working with us. There's a time in every man's life when he has to evolve. Move on. It's our time to do that."

Trace shook his head. "I'm not there yet," he said. "I told Harry he's got me for good. He's happy."

Harry King was their supervisor, a brilliant man who managed these missions like a deadly game of chess. Trace, Reed, Beau, Marcos and the rest of the team were his knights, bishops, and pawns. In fact, Trace stood up and shouted to Marcos about contacting Harry and Marcos waved him off, signaling that he already had.

As the sea spray swirled around them and the American warship came into view, the men from the unit unofficially deemed the Unholy Angels knew that their time was drawing to a close. Their last mission together. Their last time together, as least as working colleagues.

Trace looked up at the pair of them.

"It's been a hell of a ride, boys," he said, reaching out to shake Beau's hand. "And a hell of a privilege."

Beau took the extended hand and held it tightly. "Same," he said. "We won't lose touch, Trace. Don't worry. We'll be keeping tabs on you and Marcos and the rest of the guys. Just know that if you need us—anytime, anywhere—we'll be here for you."

Trace smiled weakly. "Even with guns in the middle of Tajikistan?"

Beau snorted. "Probably not," he said. "But we'll wish you well. And...and take care of yourself, Trace. You're a crazy son-of-a-bitch sometimes. It would devastate me if something happened to you."

Trace chuckled softly. "Not me," he said. "I'm too much of a sinner to die. At least, that's what my mom says. She doesn't even know half of it."

Beau grinned, patting him on the shoulder as Reed came to him, his brown eyes glittering.

"We do," Reed said, shaking his hand. "We know the half and the whole of it and you *are* mortal, so no dying on us. Why not come up to Wyoming and work with me? My dad's got a spot for you."

"As a cop?" Trace said thoughtfully. Then, he shrugged. "Maybe. I think it's more than likely I'll end up with my dad's company."

"Building things?"

"Exactly. Far, far away from this shit."

He gestured to the ship around them. The death, the destruction, the chaos. They were closing in on the American vessel and Trace finally stood up, standing with Beau and Reed as they loomed closer. Soaking up the last few moments of this mission, of time spent with the best agents he'd ever worked with. It was a damn shame they were leaving the agency, but he understood.

He had to.

Not like he had a choice.

The small craft finally met up with the warship and after that, the men were too busy to discuss last missions or futures. It was all-business, even when they had dinner with the captain and crashed in their assigned bunks. The ship made it to Marseille, where Trace, Reed, Beau, and Marcos disembarked with their prisoner and were met by members of the US Embassy in France. They transferred their captive over to the justice department and, at that point, their orders were to fly back to Washington, DC.

Mission over.

And what a mission it had been.

In particular, they would remember drinking at the airport bar at de Gaulle before the flight home. The pledges that were made, the people that were slandered, and the amount of shots they did that caused those things. On the plane home, all they did was sleep and when they awoke in DC, it was to a new day, a new dynamic, and in the case of Beau and Reed, a new life. *All good things come to an end*, Trace said.

But not really.

They would always be the good guys and damn proud of it, but more than that, they formed a brotherhood like no other. Men that had faced danger and death together. There was no getting away from it.

Or each other.

The Unholy Angels were bonded for life.

ONE
PASADENA, CALIFORNIA, EARLY OCTOBER, PRESENT DAY

IT WAS A BEAST OF A HOUSE.

Well, not exactly a beast, but it was definitely a massive project in the making. It was called a California Mission Revival style and it was built in 1895 on the corner of what had been a major section in a fashionable part of Pasadena, California back at the turn of the century. The entire area was littered with old Victorians and California Craftsman homes, so unique and indigenous to the city known as the Crown of the Valley.

Since the 1960s, the area had gradually seen a decline when it had been a hotbed of gangs. Only within the past fifteen years had the area seen change when young families began moving in, seeing the beauty in the run-down old homes and restoring them to their magnificent beauty.

Pasadena was, once again, reclaiming her family neighborhoods.

As Katharine "Kiki" Wickham-Conrad sat in the

sitting room of the massive but run-down home she had purchased, she sincerely prayed that she hadn't made a bad decision. Kiki had been born and raised in Pasadena and she knew the area extremely well, knowing that certain neighborhoods could be dicey at times, but her friend at the Pasadena Police Department assured her that her particular street was cleaning up.

The house itself sat on over a quarter of an acre, a massive lot strewn with hundred-year-old oaks that was lodged in the tightly-packed residential area. A big fence and hedge surrounded it, protecting it from the outside world. From the street, it looked like the creepy, old house where the neighborhood hermit lived. That's what Kiki had liked best about it. So, she'd bought it after much deliberation and consultation with her father and brother. Her brother had been against it but her dad had been surprisingly supportive. Her dad had been around the day that escrow closed and Kiki already had three construction companies over at the house to give her an estimate.

That had been a week ago. This morning, the construction companies were dropping by to deliver the bad news. She'd already seen two out of the three estimates and they were a lot more than she'd anticipated. Sitting in the kitchen that was stuck in the gloomy back roads of the 1950's, she begrudgingly awaited the third estimate. He said he'd be by around noon and it was almost that now.

She heard a car door slam outside. It was close enough that she suspected it was the third estimator. Kiki slid off the kitchen stool and made her way to the door like a prisoner making her way to the executioner. Based on the nauseating prices she saw that morning, this one promised to be just as gut-turning.

Maybe she should have listened to her brother. If she received one more astronomical estimate, she was going to have to consider shutting down the project before it even got started. The real estate agent who had sold her the house fed her some bullshit about the house not being in such terrible shape and, therefore, not too terribly expensive to restore, but the truth had been something quite different.

Therefore, Kiki wasn't looking forward to the third and last estimate. As she gazed at the old walls and vintage fixtures original to the house, she still saw what had attracted her to the house in the first place. All of that history right there in front of her, walls that had seen the sinking of the Titanic, World War I, the Great Depression, World War II, and all of the other significant events of the last century. But it still stood, tall and proud, as if nothing could knock it down, not even those events that had seen worlds changed and destroyed. She saw something solid and lasting.

Much as she wanted to be solid and lasting, too.

She saw hope.

The old gate creaked outside as someone entered the yard. She could hear the iron gate swing back on its hinges. *Here it comes*, she thought grimly. She had no choice now but to face the inevitable. She was already preparing the speech to give her parents on how the house was too expensive for her to keep and she'd been stupid to want to try. But the truth was that in that house, she saw something that needed her as much as she needed it. The house needed her help to shine again and, in a sense, she needed the house for the same reason. She was afraid of facing an empty future and the house was something to fill it.

More noise in the yard. Her dog at her feet barked at the sounds. She glanced at the cream-colored French Bulldog and pointed to the dog's bed, which was back in the old kitchen. Obediently, the dog trotted off as she went for the ancient bronze doorknob that was original to the house. In fact, the entire front door was original to the house. But she paused before opening it, thinking that maybe she'd just take a peek out of the window to see who it was. Maybe she didn't even feel like opening the door.

Maybe it was better if she didn't.

Making her way to the window nearest the door, she cracked open the old shutters that someone had installed forty years ago. Light suddenly poured in from the outside, filling the front parlor. In the sunlight streaming through the heavy canopy of trees around the property, she saw a figure out by the old fountain in the front yard.

The light fell upon the figure, illuminating him, as if the heavens had opened up to emphasize the man now lingering by the antique water feature. Sunlight glinted off his blond hair, his back to her. Still, she could see him and her interest grew.

The man milled around the fountain for a moment before turning toward the house. She couldn't really see his face because of the way the sun was shining but she could certainly see his figure. He was hunky; that much she knew. Nice legs and she liked the way his hair was cut. Suddenly, opening the front door seemed like a good idea.

The man had a folder in his hand so she knew he was the contractor and just not some random guy who had wandered into her yard. Moving away from the window, she went to the front door and jerked it open on its sticky hinges.

It was a moment Kiki would remember for the rest of her life.

TWO

HIS DAD SHOULD HAVE LISTENED to him.

As Trace sat outside the massive California Mission Revival structure that looked like something out of "The Munsters," he wasn't sure he even wanted to go in. He could just tell his dad that he delivered the estimate but they didn't get the job and be done with it. But, knowing his dad, the man would follow up with the owners of the house and Trace would get caught in his lie, so he emitted a grunt of frustration as he turned the truck off and bailed out.

This was the life he lived now.

He was parked on the curb outside of the home. Going around to the passenger door, he glanced up at the mammoth structure as he opened the door and pulled out the estimate folder. It was a clear day, the *Santa Ana* winds blowing away the smog and kicking up the leaves of October. Slamming the truck door with his trusty folder in-hand, he hit the remote lock and headed to the gate as the truck alarm beeped behind him.

As he opened the old, creaking gate of aged wrought iron, he glanced at his watch and thought about how quickly he could be done with this. He'd told his father a million times that Rocklin Construction was better off with the larger jobs off of the Dodge sheet. They'd gotten three very large jobs off of it over the past seven months, mostly with Trace driving the estimators like a wagon master, whip and all. These home renovations weren't worth the money, but they were something that Rocklin had built their business on, so his father was less apt to let them go. Besides, everyone in Pasadena knew Rocklin Construction and he liked to keep up that friendly, "hometown" image. Trace was trying to transition them into bigger projects while his dad, like his dad before him, leaned toward the smaller, residential ones.

Trace glanced around the yard as he headed to the front door, noting the overgrown landscaping that had once been glorious in days gone by. There was an enormous fountain with broken-out tile in and around it, like the types of Spanish-style fountains one could find at various missions. It must have been an impressive sight when it was working. Trace paused next to it, peering closely at the works and thinking that the fountain itself must be original to the house. It was ancient, begging to be restored.

With a heavy sigh, he found himself looking at the yard surrounding the fountain, which then led his attention to the porch, which was a testament to peeling paint, leaning floorboards and turn of the century construction. He flipped open the estimate folder and took a look at what they had budgeted for the porch. When he came across the number, he shook his head because it wasn't going to be enough. He could already see that.

Out of curiosity, he looked at the landscaping number and knew that wasn't going to be enough, either. In fact, the entire estimate was low. He hadn't really looked at it until this moment because this was the first time he'd seen the house. His dad had done the estimate. Frustrated, he slapped the folder shut and was about to turn away when the sound of a door opening caught his attention.

Like a fly in a trap, he was caught.

And when he saw the face of the woman who was doing the trapping, he didn't mind much in the least.

THREE

KIKI SAW the man with the folder in his hand, looking rather surprised when he saw her in the doorway.

"Hello?" she said politely.

The man's eyes widened when she spoke, as if startled. As Kiki stepped out onto the porch and the sunlight shifted again, the man's features came into view and she found herself looking at a guy who would have been better suited on a movie screen. A cursory three-second examination determined him to be a fairly gorgeous male specimen hanging around by her fountain.

Good thing I opened the door....

"Hi," he said, smiling politely.

Kiki came off the porch, heading in his direction, but the truth was that she was a little startled and more than a little star-struck. He was a good deal taller than her five feet and four inches, so much so that as she drew close to him, she realized her head only came to his chest. He had dark blond hair, cut in that stylish messy-cropped style that was so damn sexy, and his features were even and proportionate set within a granite jaw. He had rather lush lips.

But it was his eyes that had her attention; they were smoldering and intelligent. She couldn't describe it any better than that. All she knew was that she couldn't take her eyes off of them, or off of him.

"Can I help you?" she asked, extending her hand to him. "I own the house. Are you from Rocklin Construction?"

Trace took her hand and shook it. It was supple and warm. The truth was that he was finding it difficult to speak at the moment. He'd been startled by her appearance, a woman with long, dark hair shrouded in the shadows of the old porch, but the moment she came into the light, he'd been rather stunned by what he saw. Like a moth to flame, he'd been sucked in by the sweet face and big, blue eyes in a lightning-fast instant. The closer she came, the more speechless he felt at all of that beauty staring back at him. But she had asked a question and he was struggling to form an answer.

"Yes," he said, releasing her hand. "I'm here to deliver a bid."

Kiki grinned, wriggling her well-shaped eyebrows. "Uh-oh," she sighed dramatically. "Wait a minute—let me go inside and get the smelling salts."

Trace grinned; he couldn't help himself. "Do you want to sit down while I deliver the bad news?"

She laughed softly and he was utterly, instantly

entranced. "I think I'd probably better *lay* down if you're asking that question." She threw a thumb in the direction of the house. "Let me find a couch before you start talking."

Trace laughed in return, unable to help himself. "Want me to call 911 now or should I wait and see how this pans out?"

"Is it that bad?"

"I guess that depends what side of the bid you're on— the giving end or the receiving end."

Kiki put her hands on her face in horror, but she was still giggling. The man made her feel giddy as hell and she'd only known him all of ten seconds. She didn't even know his name.

"That's okay," she assured him, sobering a little. "I'm Kiki Conrad, by the way. I didn't introduce myself. I just said I'm the owner like that defines my role in life."

His grin remained. "Not a bad role if you can get it, I suppose," he said, but he sobered as well and his eyes glittered at her. "Trace Rocklin. Nice to meet you."

Her brown eyes twinkled. "Lucky me. I get one of *the* Rocklins to deliver the bad news."

"One of them," he agreed, thinking that he was, in fact, the lucky one here. "My dad had another appointment and couldn't make it to deliver the bid, so I'm the substitute."

Not a bad substitute, she thought. *Trace Rocklin.* That name brought back memories from the cobweb of her teenage years. Trace had been a friend of her older brother but she didn't remember much about the man because those were the years when she and her brother hated each other. That included hating his friends. Too bad, too. She was coming to wish she'd paid a little more attention to the big, strong, and rather silent Trace Rocklin. The boy had grown into a smoking-hot man.

Kiki's gaze lingered on him a moment, wondering if she should say anything to him about past acquaintances before deciding it was better off unsaid. If he hadn't yet made the correlation, then she wasn't going to point it out. She gestured toward the house.

"Well, come on inside and lay it on me," she said. "Might as well get it over with."

Trace had never in his life gone so willingly with someone. Forgotten were thoughts of heading back to his truck and leaving altogether. As he followed her across the walk and to the front door, he found himself checking out her curvaceous silhouette, narrow waist, and gorgeous backside. The woman had a killer butt tucked up into a pair of tight jeans. In fact, everything about her was killer. The long hair that tumbled down her back was shiny and soft-looking. He resisted the urge to reach out and touch it.

But he was jolted from is rather dirty thoughts as she opened the front door, stepping aside to usher him in. Then he was further distracted as the smell of dust, old wood, and moth balls hit him full-on. He found himself looking at a cavernous parlor with an equally massive second parlor beyond. There was a fireplace dividing the rooms, an enormous piece of work complete with exquisite

Batchelder tiles. It was a typical Pasadena older home, so unique in architecture and style to the area.

"Wow," he said, looking around. "This is quite a tomb."

Kiki's gaze followed his as she grinned. "That's exactly what this place is. A tomb. You should see the rest of it. I swear you'd think Dr. Frankenstein is going to walk from the walls at any moment."

He chuckled. "Creepy?"

"I sleep with garlic and a crucifix. What does that tell you?"

His laughter grew. "That you probably chase your husband from bed with the smell."

She didn't even stop to think that it might have been a leading question, which it was, but Trace had worked it into the conversation so beautifully that she hadn't noticed. She threw up her hands for emphasis.

"There's no self-respecting husband on earth that would have let his wife buy a tomb like this," she said. "I don't have one, anyway, so it doesn't really matter. Come on into the kitchen so you can give me the bad news. Sorry, but there's nowhere else to sit right now."

So she wasn't married, which made him feel strangely happy. Then he became angry at himself because he shouldn't have had any reaction one way or the other, nor should he have even made the leading statement, but it had all happened so fast. He was feeling rather upswept by her, losing control of his usually controlled senses.

Following the woman's lovely round bottom through what was presumably the massive dining room and into the ancient kitchen by way of a narrow butler's pantry, he noticed that the pantry was lined with hundred-year-old cabinetry. It was truly something to see, smelling as old and musty as it possibly could.

The kitchen had sixty-year-old fixtures and tile that was at least that old. He looked down at the old linoleum, which at one time would have been the height of fashion. It seemed like such a sad, old place, like a former movie star begging for someone to help her shine again. He could almost hear the pleas.

"This place must have really been a showplace in its day," he commented.

Kiki sat on one of two wooden stools in the room, shoved up against the old kitchen counter. Her gaze followed his as he inspected the room.

"It was," she replied. "I've done some research on it through the Pasadena Historical Society. The home was built in 1895 by Mr. Austin Glen, an Atchison, Topeka and Santa Fe railroad executive who has a street named after him somewhere around here. Anyway, he was friends with the Greene and Greene brothers, who are so iconic in Pasadena, so they designed this house for him, although it's not the traditional Greene and Greene Craftsman. It has Mission elements in it because Mr. Glen wanted something with more California Spanish influence. His family lived here for about twenty years, whereupon they sold it to a silent movie actress who really turned it into a showplace. Back then, the house sat on about three acres of land and she had stables and ponds and even a giant swimming pool, all of which are gone now. There were stories about the wild parties she would throw here and then get the cops drunk when they showed up to bust it up. But she died in the nineteen sixties and the house apparently has seen a steady decline since then."

By this time, he was listening to her story with interest. He smiled faintly as he sat down on the stool next to her.

"And now you have it," he said, putting the estimating folder on the counter. "Planning on any wild parties like the old movie star did?"

She laughed, displaying perfect teeth. "Not so much," she said. "I think my partying days are over. I'm little old for that."

He shot her an expression, gently done, that suggested she was crazy. "I don't believe that for a minute," he said, then thought it sounded too much like a compliment and, not wanting to obviously flirt with the woman any more than he already had, he somewhat nervously changed the subject. "Well, it's quite a project, anyway."

Kiki nodded, conceding the point. Trace was sitting next to her now, at close range, and her heart was beginning to race at his proximity. At this range, she could see that he had hazel eyes that were almost a dark gold color and they gazed back at her with curiosity and warmth. The guy was unbelievably handsome and it was a struggle for her to keep her head on straight.

"Okay," she said, pretending to brace herself against the kitchen counter. "I'm sitting down. Lay it on me."

He laughed softly at her sense of humor, something

he'd seen nearly the moment they started talking. She was very animated and bright, something he found incredibly attractive. He was starting to think obviously flirting with her wasn't such a bad idea.

"Here it comes," he said, tearing his eyes away from her and focusing on the folder. "Ready?"

"Ready."

"Do you want a breakdown or an overall total?"

She shrugged. "Better cut to the chase. The overall total."

Even as he looked at the numbers, he was reminded that they weren't right. As he'd suspected from the beginning, the number was so low that it was ridiculous. He had no idea what his dad was thinking when he worked up the estimate, but he might have been thinking the same thing Trace was—that Kiki Conrad was a very beautiful woman and, somehow, that earned her the beautiful woman discount.

His dad was rather a softy, especially after his mom passed away three years before. Dad was lonely. Maybe Ms. Conrad had turned on the charm in the hopes of getting a better deal. She'd certainly been very flirty with Trace and it began to occur to him why. Not knowing the woman at all, her character or moral compass, his sense of self-protection began to kick in. Maybe she was trying to work him, too.

He'd learned long ago not to trust anyone.

Especially women.

"The overall total for the complete restoration of the

house and grounds is two hundred and forty-three thou-sand," he said, businesslike. "That's just for what we know about; however, as you discover in construction, there are things that pop up all over the place and then a change order would have to be signed. That would increase your costs. Who knows what we'll find when we start digging into the walls."

Kiki could sense his change in manner almost immedi-ately. He'd gone from warm and funny to rather stiff and formal, as if a switch were suddenly thrown. It had all happened the moment he'd looked at that folder and she wondered why. But because he seemed so stiff, she felt a little uncertain. That, and the fact that he'd just slammed her with a rather large bid. Her good mood was gone. She sat back on the stool, her expression a mixture of resigna-tion and disappointment. The fun and games of the past few minutes were definitely over.

"Oh," she finally said. "Well, that's more than I'd hoped it would be even though that's the lowest bid of the day. You said that includes the grounds?"

He looked up from the folder, fixing her in the eye. "Yes," he replied. "But I have to be honest and tell you that even though we budgeted about twenty thousand for the yard, I don't think it's going to be enough. You've got a hell of a lot of work out there to do and this is just the bare bones."

Kiki was coming to suspect he was talking her out of accepting his bid. She didn't know why, but something in his manner just gave off those vibes. He was beginning to come across impatient, as if he had better things to be doing. It was all very strange, considering things had been fine when they had first met. She began to review their brief conversation in her mind, wondering what she could have said to offend him, because that's what he was acting like. Evidently, somehow or someway, she had offended him. Instinctively, she backed down. It was clear that, for whatever reason, he didn't even want the job.

"I see," she replied to his statement, her manner uncertain yet still friendly. "It's certainly a lot to think about. I guess I really didn't know what to expect when I bought this place, so now I know."

His gaze lingered on her, noticing that her manner was far more subdued as well. He realized he was rather sorry to see that. He'd really liked her animated and funny personality. He was starting to feel confused and guilty about the whole thing.

"Homes like this really are kind of a beast," he said, easing somewhat. "I guess you really had no way of knowing until you're right in the middle of it. It'll be a beautiful place when it's done, but that's going to cost."

She nodded, looking pensive and thoughtful. She hung her head, looking at her feet as she pondered his statement. Then she shrugged her shoulders and stood up.

"Well," she said, "I guess I have a lot to think about. How long is your bid valid?"

"Thirty days."

"Can I please have a copy?"

"Sure." He yanked a sheet of paper out of the folder, forgetful, and handed it to her. "This is your copy."

"Thanks."

He watched her as she looked over the numbers, coming to feel like a jerk for being so hard with her when she'd really done nothing to deserve it. His old and familiar insecurities had gotten the better of him, inbred suspicions that had been his constant companion for years. Women had always been something, as a species, that had him on his guard. That inherent suspicion had always served him well, keeping him alive and out of trouble, but he suspected that wasn't the case today. It began to occur to him that he was so greatly torn because he was very attracted to her. He didn't want her flirty, sparkly personality to be a ruse. He wanted it to be real.

"Do you have any questions?" he asked, somewhat gently.

Kiki was looking at all of the giant numbers on the sheet. After a couple of moments, she glanced up at him. "Is there anything on here that absolutely, positively doesn't have to be done? Something that can wait?"

He flipped open his folder to look at the same bid sheet she was looking at. "Well," he said slowly, "if you don't mind just doing one thing at a time, it can all be done in pieces, but you will have to do plumbing and electrical first to bring the place up to code. Does any of it work now?"

She nodded, studying the estimate in her hand intently. "The master bathroom works for the most part and the kitchen, living and dining rooms all have power. I can live here, at any rate, but I'll have to put my other plans on hold, I guess."

He looked up from the folder. "What plans?"

She pointed to the estimate sheet. "See all of the bathrooms I was planning on renovating?" she asked. "I'm going to turn this place into a bed and breakfast and also a wedding venue. I figured why not? It's a great location, and Pasadena has become a mecca for that kind of thing. It would be the opportunity to make some money."

He nodded. "With a place like this, that's a good idea."

She glanced up at him. "The house sits on almost an acre and even though everything is overgrown, there's that gorgeous antique fountain in the front and that spectacular side yard. Well, at least it will be spectacular when I'm finished with it. But that fountain is the best feature on the entire property. I think it would be a great place for people to get married."

Trace glanced around the room. "With a big, old house like this, I think you'd have it made," he said. "People really love intimate venues like this."

Kiki nodded, her gaze still on the estimate sheet. "That's what I thought," she said. "I think the location is perfect because of the house's proximity to Old Town Pasadena and to the Rose Bowl, but I was kind of hoping that the revenue from the bed and breakfast would help pay for...well, anyway, I guess it doesn't matter. I'll figure it out."

He was still pondering the wedding venue idea. "I was

wondering why you were having every bathroom re-done," he admitted. "I just thought you had a lot of kids."

She grinned. "Just two girls, both in their first year in college," she said. "I was going to turn the big attic into their space. See it on the sheet?"

He nodded, his focus on the part of the bid that estimated the build-out of the attic space. "Yes," he replied. "That build-out isn't going to be cheap because of the bathroom you're adding up there."

"I'm coming to think bathrooms, in general, are very expensive."

"Yes, they sure are."

She fell silent, her gaze still on the bid sheet and the disappointing information contained therein. It seemed like the conversation was coming to a dead end and Trace wasn't sure what more to say to her. He'd been kind of a jerk for the last few minutes and was coming to feel very torn and guilty about the whole thing. Just as he was thinking about calling it quits because he couldn't think of anything else to say, he noticed something down by his feet. Looking down, he saw a cream-colored, flat-faced dog looking up at him.

"Hey, dog," he muttered.

Kiki glanced up from the bid and saw who he was talking to. "That's Stanley."

"Is he friendly?"

"He'll lick you to death before you know what hit you."

He crouched down, scratching the dog on the top of the head. "What kind of dog is he?"

"French Bulldog." She finally set the bid sheet on the counter and faced him. "I don't want to keep you any longer because I'm sure you're very busy, so thanks very much for delivering the bid. And I appreciate you taking the time to answer my questions honestly."

He stopped scratching the dog and stood up, looking her in the eye. He could feel himself growing soft again, relenting, thinking that he'd been an ass. He'd judged the woman before he even knew her, using old prejudices as justification. All pretty women were the same...*weren't they?*

"You're welcome," he said, turning in the direction of the front door because she was. "If you have any more questions about the bid, don't hesitate to call."

Kiki walked past him on her way to the front of the house. "I won't," she said. "But I think receiving three mammoth bids in one day tells me that I maybe need to re-think this whole renovation thing."

Trace followed her and the dog as they made their way back to the front room. "Like I said, it doesn't have to be all at once," he told her as they crossed from the dining room into the front room with the massive fireplace. "You may want to think about just doing it in pieces; you know, the most important parts first."

She nodded seriously. "I'll definitely think about it," she replied as they reached the front door and she opened it for him. When their eyes met, she forced a smile. "Thank you again for coming. I really appreciate it."

He just looked at her, forcing a rather weak smile in

return because he was feeling like such a lout about everything. "You're welcome."

For lack of anything more to say about the whole thing, he walked out onto the porch with Kiki right behind him. She paused on the porch steps as he continued on, heading toward the massive antique fountain. Kiki watched his big body as he moved, his broad shoulders and masculine lines. He also had a great ass, something that drew her attention more than it should have. Too bad she had offended him and chased him off with whatever she must have said. She knew she was going to spend a lot of time pondering that dilemma.

He paused by the fountain, turning to look at it and distracting her view of his butt. She saw where he was looking. In fact, when she first saw him, he had been gazing at the fountain. It must have held some interest for him.

"I didn't see what your bid said about the fountain," Kiki said. "It's original to the house, you know. It's one hundred and twenty-something years old. I'd sure like to see it work again. It's so much a part of this house."

Trace looked at her. "It's prominent, that's for sure."

She shook her head and moved closer. "I meant that the fountain actually identifies the house," she said. "Austin Glen named the house *Agua de la Vida* after the mythical location of the Fountain of Youth. Presumably, this fountain is representative of that and it's important to me that it be restored. I want it to be the best feature here."

He smiled faintly. "Did you tell my dad that? About the fountain, I mean. He likes old stories like that."

Kiki shook her head. "I didn't tell your dad anything."

"Why not?"

"Because I've never met him."

He looked at her, both confused and surprised. "You haven't? But..."

"My dad was here the day your dad came to do the estimate," she told him, cutting him off. "Whatever was discussed was between the two of them and I don't remember if my dad told me if they discussed the fountain."

I've never met him.

So she didn't get the beautiful woman discount. Trace stared at her, feeling as awful as he possibly could. He'd jumped to conclusions and, like an idiot, got what he deserved. He was ashamed and embarrassed. This beautiful, sexy, and funny woman whom he felt more attraction to in the first few minutes of knowing her than he'd ever felt for anyone in his life was innocent of what he'd mentally accused her of. He began to seriously backpedal, wondering how he could mend the damage, not because he wanted the job but because he felt like he needed to make amends to her.

"Tell you what," he said after a moment. "Why don't you walk me around the place and let *me* do the estimate based on what *you* want. Maybe I can shave some of this down. Maybe I can't. But it's worth a try. I'm starting to think maybe my dad got his signals crossed or something, because this bid didn't look right to me from the start."

She seemed to perk up. "Really? Why would you say that?"

He didn't want to tell her that he thought it was way too low. It seemed like he wanted to make it up to her for his turncoat behavior - friendly to her one minute, an ass to her the next.

Maybe the truth was that he just didn't want to leave.

"I'm not sure," he said, shrugging as he looked around the dead yard that had been a real showplace in days gone by. "I think maybe I'd better give this a shot myself. Maybe I'll come up with something my dad didn't."

The light came back into those beautiful eyes. "That would be great," she agreed. "Are you sure you have time right now?"

His expression took on a warm glimmer again, the one she'd seen when they'd first met.

"I'll make the time."

FOUR

"WHAT'S WRONG?" came the voice. "You look like a man in agony."

Trace glanced up from his computer, seeing his brother, Jesse, standing in the door to his office. He grinned at his younger brother by twenty-two months as he took off his glasses, set them on his desk, and leaned back in his chair.

"I'm working on redoing that estimate for the Conrad property," he said. "I thought I could pare down some of the costs but it's just not looking good. That place needs utter and complete restoration and, as it is, we're going to have to call in the State of California and the City of Pasadena because it's a historical structure. It was awarded historic status about twenty years ago. I sense a nightmare coming."

Jesse Rocklin made a distasteful face. "Blow it off," he said. "Tell them we just can't do it."

Trace didn't want to let his brother in on what he was thinking—that spending the half hour yesterday with Kiki Conrad walking the house and gathering information for a new bid had been perhaps one of the better half hours of his life. She had been flirty and vivacious, but they had strictly talked about the house and nothing else. He'd left there determined to work up a new bid that was more attractive than the last, but so far, he just couldn't seem to make it work. His vendors weren't cooperating as he'd hoped.

"I can't," he sighed. "I promised her I'd give it another shot."

Jesse cocked his head. "Her? Her who?"

Trace laced his fingers behind his head and leaned back in his chair. "Kiki Conrad. The owner."

Jesse just looked confused until a second or two later, realization dawned. "Oh, yes," he said. "I remember. Dad knows her parents. They go to the same church."

Trace's eyebrows rose. "Really?" he said. "He didn't mention that."

Jesse nodded. "He said something about it the other day," he said. "When he was working on the bid. I asked him why he was bothering with it and he told me. Also, we went to school with their son, who I would presume is Kiki Conrad's brother."

Trace was growing more surprised. "We did? Who?"

"Remember Jimmy Wickham?"

Trace's eyes widened. "Jimmy Wickham is her brother?" He sat forward in his chair, his mouth popping open. "*That's* Jim's little sister?"

"I'm pretty sure she is. Conrad must be her married name."

Trace was astounded. "Oh, my God," he hissed, thinking back to his teenage years when James Wickham had been part of his circle of friends. "Jim and I played football together for four years in high school. I remember going to his house and I remember his little sister, but he always called her 'runt'. I don't even think I knew her name."

Jesse nodded to the recollections. "I was in her grade but she went to Pasadena High School while we all went to the all-boys Catholic school," he said. "I remember Dad saying that she was living somewhere down in Orange County until her husband died about a year ago. Now she's back up here and bought some old derelict house to restore."

Trace was still digesting the fact that he knew the family. "That's an understatement," he muttered. "You should see the place. It's straight out of the horror movies."

"She never said that she knew us?"

"Not a word."

Jesse nodded and started to reply, but the receptionist flagged him down with a phone call. "So now you know why Dad gave these people the rock star treatment," he said, turning away from the office door. "I've got to take this call."

Trace let his brother go, thinking about Jim Wickham

and his skinny little sister, or at least what he remembered of her. That skinny little girl grew up to be a goddess of chestnut-colored hair and sexy blue eyes.

He should have paid more attention.

In fact, he couldn't get her off his mind as he finished up the bid. He had been waiting for a drywall guy to call him back, one that specialized in the lathe and plaster of older walls, and then he spent a half hour trying to talk the guy down by promising him the job on another bid he was working on. Hanging up the phone, he spent another half hour reworking the numbers and all he could do was chop about fifty thousand off the original bid. It wasn't much, but it was something.

Chewing on breath mints and running a comb through his hair, he got into his truck and headed for West Pasadena.

It was a fairly warm day outside, the dry winter season of Southern California that could sometimes be hotter than the summers. Trees were still green, though sagging for lack of water, and the San Gabriel Mountains were turning dead shades of brown. A light breeze hinted at the cool season it should have been.

Trace parked his truck in front of the house, feeling a bit nervous. He felt like he was getting ready to go out on a first date with a woman he really wanted to see. The truth was that he really wanted to see Kiki Conrad and hadn't called her first before coming over because he didn't want her to somehow discourage him from coming. Maybe she wanted her bad news over the phone this time. But he was here now, so he'd deliver it in person and maybe even get to comfort her if it was worse than she'd expected.

Climbing out of the truck, he collected the folder from the seat and shut the door. Opening the old wrought iron gate, he stepped back in time into that world of overgrown gardens and ancient fountain. As he made his way to the front door, he heard a voice off to his right.

"Hello there."

He turned to see Kiki partially hidden in the shrubbery. She had a big gardening hat on and her hands were covered by gloves. On closer inspection, he could see garden tools all around her and piles of cut limbs, leaves, and weeds. It was apparent that she had been very busy. She was flushed in the face, smiling at him as their eyes met. He smiled back.

"Dr. Livingston, I presume?" he asked.

She burst out laughing. "That's what I feel like," she said, making her way out of the bushes. "I swear this place is so overgrown that it's going to take me years to shape this yard up. Good thing I like to garden."

She came close and he reached out, pulling a particularly large cobweb off her hat that was trailing down over her shoulder. They both snickered when he tore it down and tossed it aside, with Kiki taking a healthy step away from it.

"You didn't happen to see the spider that came from, did you?" she asked.

He shook his head. "I did not," he looked around behind her and up in the trees. "But he'll probably be hard to miss."

"I'm feeling scared and threatened right now."

"You should."

They started laughing again, a spark of warmth igniting between them. It had threatened to spark yesterday before Trace backed off and acted like a jerk, but today, he wasn't afraid to let it ignite. He welcomed it.

"So what brings you to the jungle today?" Kiki finally asked. "Don't tell me you're finished with the bid already?"

He nodded. "I told you that I'd get back to you as quick as I could."

Kiki smiled up at him with her flushed cheeks, pulling off her gloves. "You really could have called. You didn't have to drive all the way over here."

"No problem," he said. "I was in the neighborhood."

She accepted his explanation even though it was a flat-out lie. "Great," she said. "Let's go inside and get away from the spiders."

"Sure."

He followed her toward the porch, watching her butt again just because he liked it so much. She was dressed in casual khaki pants, a little baggy, but even the loose material couldn't disguise her great figure. She was also wearing a tank top, showing much more skin than she had the previous day, with the bonus view of a great pair of breasts because the shirt was rather clingy. *She sure didn't look like this when we were teenagers because I definitely would have noticed.*

"Whew," she sighed as she opened the big front door. "I didn't realize how hot it was out there. Isn't it October?"

"Last time I checked," he said, stepping into the cool entry. "It's nice in here."

She wriggled her eyebrows. "One of the advantages of those high ceilings," she said, pointing upward and he instinctively looked up. "I don't imagine it really gets hot in here even on super-hot days."

"Probably not," he agreed. He opened his mouth to say more but was distracted by the fat French Bulldog trotting up to him from the kitchen. He gave the dog a half-hearted salute. "Hey, Bullfrog."

Kiki giggled. "It's Stanley."

"I know. But he looks like a bullfrog."

She laughed. "Did you drive all the way over here just to insult my dog?"

He grinned. "That's an insult? I thought it was a fact."

She continued laughing and pulled off the hat, leaving a delightfully mussed ponytail in its wake. Trace stared at her, thinking he'd never seen such a beautiful woman, mussed hair and all.

"Before you destroy my dog's self-confidence with your insults, why don't you tell me what's on that sheet of paper you have," she pointed to the folder. "I'm hoping it's good news."

He flipped open the folder even though he knew what the bid said down to the last detail. "It's better than it was before," he said, although there was caution in his tone. "Do you want the overall number or do you want me to go through it line item by line item?"

"Overall number," she said as she turned for the kitchen. "Can I offer you something to drink while we do this?"

"Sure," he said.

"Water or soda?"

"Water's fine, thanks."

By that time they had reached the ancient kitchen and Kiki opened up the refrigerator that looked like it was second hand, like something she'd gotten on clearance somewhere. She extended a cold bottle of water to him and took one for herself. Twisting off the cap, she took a long drink before speaking.

"Here we go with Round Two," she grinned at him. "What's the damage now?"

Trace set the bottle of water down on the counter and handed her a copy of the bid. "I was able to get it down to one hundred and eighty-nine thousand," he said. "I had to call in a few favors, but I think we can get the place mostly restored for that. The only thing it doesn't include is a tear-down of the garage. We're just going to have to basically rebuild it to bring it up to code because I called the Pasadena Building Department and they told me that since the garage was older than fifty years, we can't tear it down unless it's a hazard, which it's not. Since it's part of the original complex of the house, they'd fight you on it if you tried to tear it down. It's considered a historical structure."

Kiki was looking at the sheet of paper in front of her. Trace could see from her expression that she wasn't entirely thrilled with the new bid. She was trying to hide her disappointment but couldn't quite manage it.

"I think the garage originally housed wagons and stuff," she said, her voice sounding oddly small and forlorn. She continued reading the bid for a couple of seconds longer before looking up at Trace. "I really appreciate you doing this a second time. You really did a lot...you know, shaving off some of the costs, and...well, it looks...less. I really need to sit down and go over everything and talk it over with my accountant."

Trace was a fairly intuitive guy. He could see that the fifty thousand he'd cut from the original bid wasn't what she had hoped for.

"Absolutely," he said. "Do what you need to do and then let me know one way or the other. But can I ask a question?"

"Sure."

"When you bought the house, you knew it needed a lot of work, right?"

"Yes."

"Did you have a budget for it set aside? You know— knowing that you needed to do it. Did you have a number in mind?"

She sighed faintly, looking at the paper somewhat hesitantly before glancing down at the dog. "Hey, accountant," she said. "Did we have a number in mind?"

Stanley cocked his doggie head at her and she sighed again, catching sight of Trace from the corner of her eye and realizing he was expecting an answer. She owed it to him. He'd worked hard to pare down the bid. He deserved some kind of explanation.

"I was really hoping to keep it around eighty thousand," she finally said. "It seemed like a reasonable number when I bought the house and talked to the real estate agent about the restoration, but now hearing four bids come back at nearly four times that amount, I feel pretty stupid."

Trace twisted the top off his water. "Don't feel that way," he said. "I'm sure you didn't know what you were getting in to. Projects like this have a way of taking on a life of their own. But you should know that everything on that bid sheet is a necessary item. I didn't leave any fluff. I'm not sure where I could cut any more corners."

Kiki's gaze lingered on him for a moment. "You said you called in favors for this?" she shook the sheet. "Why on earth would you do that?"

"Because you get the old friend discount."

She stared at him a moment before she realized what he meant. Then, she broke out in a crooked grin. "So you figured it out, did you?"

He didn't look amused, but it was all for show. He tried to sound stern. "Why didn't you tell me you were Jimmy's little sister?"

She laughed softly. "How'd you guess? Did your dad tell you?"

"My brother told me. But you still haven't answered my question - why didn't *you* tell me?"

"Because I'm sure you wouldn't have remembered me from Adam," she said. "In fact, all I remember of you is this big, silent kid coming in and out of the house with my brother and a bunch of other guys he hung around with. I really only recognized your name when you showed up yesterday. If I'd passed you on the street, I never would have known you."

He scratched his chin. "So much for making an impression," he muttered, watching her snort. "I haven't talked to Jim in years. How is he?"

"Great," Kiki nodded. "He's living in San Diego now, working for a marketing company."

"Didn't you have an older sister, too?"

"Deborah," she replied. "Debbie. She's retired with her husband up in the wilds of Montana. They've got a gazillion acre ranch and a million head of cattle, or something like that. She lives like a pioneer up there."

He chuckled. "And you?" He tried to make it sound conversational, not like he was hugely interested. "What have you been doing for the past twenty-five years?"

Her good humor faded. "Happily married until last year," she said, her voice softer. "I met my husband in college when he was pre-Med. He opened up an oncology practice down in Orange County and we lived down there with our twin girls up until last year when he dropped dead of a heart attack."

Trace's smile faded as well. "I'm so sorry," he said sincerely. "That's rough."

Kiki nodded, trying not to dwell on memories that were only now starting to ease. The pain wasn't as bad as it used to be. "It was," she agreed. "But we're doing okay."

"We?"

"Me and the girls—Esme Elizabeth and Embry Alexandra. They started their first year of college a couple of months ago."

"Where are they going?"

"University of California San Diego because that's where their dad went. They both wanted to go there as a kind of tribute to him."

He could see her expression light up as she spoke of her daughters. "So the girls go to school and Mom buys a massive project to oversee," he said, watching her nod in agreement. "You sure picked a doozy."

"Is that a construction term?"

"It is. So are thingamabob, doohickey, and thinga-majigger."

They gazed at each other a moment before breaking down into soft chuckles. That warmth was there again, stronger than it had been the first time. Trace sipped at his water, taking his sweet time, looking around the kitchen as Kiki's attention went back to the bid sheet.

"What about you, Trace?" she asked, still looking at the sheet as he visually inspected a particularly old cabinet.

"What have you been up to the past twenty-five years? It looks like you stayed local if you're working for your dad."

He turned to look at her, thinking many different things at that moment. *If you only knew how completely off the mark that statement is.*

"Actually," he said casually, reaching out to touch the old and leaning cabinet. "I only came back home about a year ago myself. I'd been in Washington D.C. since I graduated from Annapolis."

She looked up from the paper. "Annapolis?" she repeated. "Were you in the military?"

"I worked for the government," he said, giving his generically standard reply. "I put in my twenty-five years and got out. I came back home to work for the family business and so far, it's been a good change."

"That's nice to hear," she said, leaning on the counter and gazing up at him with her big green eyes. "Didn't you have a couple of brothers?"

He nodded, glad they were off the subject of the past twenty-five years. He really didn't want to talk about it, *couldn't* talk about it, and he didn't want to stand there and make up lies just for the sake of conversation.

"Jesse and Shaun," he said. "They're both younger."

"You're the big brother, eh?"

"Big and scary. They still won't mess with me."

She giggled. "You don't look so scary to me."

He grinned as she laughed. "I don't *want* to look scary to you."

It was a decidedly flirtatious statement, one she

quickly succumbed to. It had been a long time since someone had openly flirted with her and although their brief acquaintances yesterday and today had been filed with flirty little moments, that statement opened the door to take it to a whole new level. He was being more obvious about it. Kiki went right along with it.

"Oh, yeah?" she cocked her head. "If you did want to look scary to me, how would you do it?"

He pointed to the paper in her hand. "Leave that bid just as it was and not try to work it down."

She grinned broadly and looked at the bid sheet. "You're an angel for doing this, but I'm seriously going to have to sit down and go over this and figure some things out."

"Fair enough," he said, sensing that perhaps the conversation was coming to a close and not wanting it to. Then he said the first thing that popped to mind, unable to stop himself. "Hey, I was just going to get some lunch. Want to join me?"

He cringed as the words left his mouth, already mentally kicking his ass all the way across the room. *Smooth, you idiot!* It had been so long since he'd met a woman he was attracted to, much less asked someone out, that he was very out of practice. The words just came spilling out before he could even think about what he was saying.

But Kiki didn't flinch. She stood up from where she had been leaning over the counter and glanced at her watch.

"Sure," she said without hesitation. "I didn't even realize what time it was. Can you give me about ten minutes to clean up?"

Trace was thrilled, trying desperately not to show it. "Sure," he waved her off. "Take your time. Me and Bullfrog will keep each other company."

He was looking down at the dog, who had taken up station by his feet, and Kiki laughed. "It's *Stanley*," she said. "You're going to give my dog an identity complex."

He just laughed, still eyeing the dog as she darted off up the back stairs to the second floor. A thought occurred to him and he went to the back stairwell where she had just disappeared, gazing up into the very dark well. He could see the dimly lit second floor beyond.

"Hey!" he called.

Her voice was distant. "Yes?"

"I just thought of something," he said loudly as it echoed up the well. "Are you actually living here?"

He received no immediate answer. Then, her face appeared at the top of the well. "Of course I am," she said. "Why?"

He cocked an eyebrow, giving her a disapproving expression. "Will you at least let me do something for you, then?"

"What?"

"Will you let me check out the electrical and plumbing to make sure it's okay since you're actually living here? If it's anything like the rest of the house, then I'm kind of scared of the thought of you flipping a switch and a wire sparking."

Kiki gazed down at him, genuinely touched by the offer. Since the moment he'd set foot back on the property, he'd been sweet, kind and concerned. She could feel herself warming to the man whether or not she really wanted to. She couldn't decide yet. But her heart, that fragile thing that had been so badly crushed by Mark's death last year, had other ideas. *A little flirt with a handsome acquaintance from the past is harmless,* she told herself. Might be good for her.

"How much will it cost me?" she asked. "I've got a tight budget, you know."

"No charge."

Her eyebrows lifted. "Really?"

"Really."

"I don't want you to think I'm taking advantage of you if I let you do it."

"I'm the one that offered.

"Well," she said somewhat hesitantly. "Okay. But don't do too much, okay? You'll make me feel guilty."

He grinned. "You finish what you're doing," he said, turning back to the kitchen. "I'll look around down here."

Kiki watched him disappear. She could hear him moving around down in the kitchen. Quickly, she ran back into the master bedroom and yanked off her clothing, running for the shower. The master bathroom was about sixty years old, with horrible peach-colored ceramic tile, a very old bathtub, and a shower enclosure with an arched entry. Still, it worked, so she turned on the water and watched it spray from the ancient showerhead that was in desperate need of replacement. Piling her hair on top of her head and clipping it, she jumped in when it got moderately warm.

It was a three-minute shower, just enough to soap down and rinse off. Climbing out, she dried off, quickly put on some lotion, and then slapped on some make-up and did her hair. It was long, with a little curl on the ends, so she just brushed it out pulled it into a ponytail. Rushing back into the bedroom, she dug out a pair of jeans and the cutest top she could find that wasn't buried deep in a box, and put them on. Having only moved into the house two weeks ago, she still had stuff in boxes.

Finishing off with a pair of wedge sandals, she took a quick look at herself and thought it wasn't a bad look for a ten-minute job. All the while, she was thinking about that gorgeous man down in her kitchen and how she felt like a girl going out on her first date. Well, it kind of *was* her first date in over twenty-five years, so it was something to be excited about. Gathering her purse, she went downstairs.

She found Trace in the kitchen with four light sockets pulled apart. He had a screwdriver in hand, dismantling a fifth light socket, and she stood there a moment and watched him concentrate.

"Well?" she asked. "Is the house going to burn down around me?"

He glanced up and she swore she saw a look of appreciation cross his features when he saw how well she cleaned up. "No," he said. "But..."

Before he could finish, something abruptly shot out of the light socket and landed on the floor. It took Kiki a moment to realize it was a mouse and she shrieked as Stanley went crazy with barking and gave chase. Kiki hopped up onto the old kitchen counter and drew her legs up, yelping, as her dog began to chase the little mouse around the kitchen.

Trace set the screwdriver down and followed the dog at a distance to see which direction the animals were going to take. Thinking quickly, he noticed a few washed dishes in the sink, one being a Tupperware container. He grabbed it and the lid, and waited until there was a shift in the winds. Stanley had managed to chase the mouse in a big circle and it was now heading back in his direction.

Trace positioned himself correctly so the mouse passed near him. At the right moment, he slammed the Tupperware down on top of the mouse, effectively trapping it, as Stanley jumped up and down on Trace's hands excitedly. He tried to be gentle about shooing the dog away as he slipped the lid under the container and sealed the mouse up.

"Crisis averted," he said, turning to Kiki with the container in his hand. "What do you want me to do with it?"

She was sitting on the counter hugging her legs against her chest, eyes wide. "Take it outside," she motioned frantically towards the utility room and the back door beyond. "Let it go outside."

Trace did as she instructed, keeping the excited dog in the house as he went outside and released his quarry. When he came back into the house, he saw that Kiki was still sitting on the counter, terrified. He set the Tupperware down and grinned at her.

"Are you going to stay there?" he asked.

"Yes."

"Forever?"

"Yes."

He laughed softly. "Can I help you down?"

She shrugged but didn't make any real effort to get down, so he went over to her and scooped her right up from the counter. It had been a chivalrous gesture that quickly turned into one of delicious surprise. He had no idea she would feel so good in his arms, but he should have. She was warm and soft, and smelled wonderful. His heart began to thump against his ribs giddily as he carried her out of the kitchen.

As soon as they hit the large entry area, she slithered out of his arms. He didn't seem to notice the faint flush to her cheeks. "Thanks for the lift," she said. "I think it's safe."

He tried not to look too disappointed that she didn't want him to carry her around. "Didn't you have this place inspected for rodents during escrow?"

She nodded, taking a deep breath and trying to blow

off the fact that his chivalrous gesture of carrying her out of the kitchen had her heart fluttering madly.

"They found a few but assured me they'd been removed," she said, pulling her sunglasses out of her purse. "I guess we need to revisit that particular issue."

Trace pulled his truck keys out of his pocket. "I think you'd better."

She put her sunglasses on. "If I don't, you'll have to add carrying me around all over the house to your restoration bid. Mice and I can't share the same floor space."

He grinned as he opened the front door. "I'll add it in but there won't be any charge. You don't weigh very much."

"I will if you have to do it sixteen hours a day."

"We'll work it out."

She chuckled as she walked past him and out onto the porch. He followed. Then, she turned to lock the door before following him out to his truck parked out by the curb. It was a nice, newer model truck and he was a gentleman, holding the door open for her as he ushered her in. Climbing into the driver's seat, he made a U-turn and headed south to the old town district of Pasadena.

FIVE

THE ENTIRE DRIVE to the old town section of Pasadena, with its high-end shops and world-class restaurants, Trace had no idea where they were truly going. He just acted like he knew so Kiki didn't think he was a complete dork. Once they hit Colorado Boulevard and he spied an upper-end café with outdoor seating, he determined that it would be their destination. He'd never been there in his life but he hoped it would be good. He just wanted to be the man with the plan.

He parked the truck in one of the four-story parking structures that was just off the main drag, politely opening Kiki's door for her and escorting her out of the structure. The weather was still very warm and dry, the sun hot if you weren't in the shade, but, all in all, it was glorious. He left his jacket in the truck as they made their way down the block.

It was mostly small talk between them, about past people they knew or her brother's girl-chasing ways in high school. He was becoming better acquainted with her truly funny sense of humor and liking it a great deal. The woman had a hell of a sparkly personality, animated and fun, which he found entrancing. By the time they reached the café and were seated, he considered himself on the border of being officially smitten. He'd never been smitten in his life.

"So," Kiki ventured after the waitress took their drink order, "what kind of name is Trace? Are you named after someone?"

He took his sunglasses off and laid them on the table. "It's short for Tracy," he said. "It's my mother's maiden name, but I absolutely hated it because in kindergarten there was a girl whose name was Tracy, also. Once I figured out it was a girl's name, too, I insisted on being called Trace."

Kiki grinned. "More manly."

"Exactly."

"Do you still hate it?"

He shrugged. "My name's Trace. That's just what it is."

"But what if I want to call you Tracy?"

"Then you're the only one I'll let call me that."

She giggled. "I'd never emasculate you like that. If you hate it, *I* hate it."

He laughed softly and sipped his water. "So what about Kiki? That's not your real name, is it?"

She settled back in her seat, grinning. She had an enormous dimple in her right cheek that Trace found very sexy.

"No," she said. "I got it from Jim. He was two when I was born and couldn't pronounce Katharine. It came out something like 'Kaki', which somehow became Kiki. And if that's not enough, my dad and my sister only call me 'Keeks'. Even my nickname has a nickname."

"What does your mother call you?"

"It depends on if she's mad at me or not. Usually it's Kiki, but if she's pissed, it's Katharine."

"Funny how those things work out."

She nodded, glancing up at the waitress as the woman brought an iced tea for Trace and a diet cola for her. The woman proceeded to take their food orders and wandered away. Kiki took a long drink of her cola.

"You said you worked for the government in Washington," she said. "What did you do?"

Trace had a standard answer for this kind of question, the same answer he'd used for twenty-five years. It wasn't the truth, but it wasn't exactly a lie, either. It was the safe answer.

"I worked for the CIA," he said. "Analyst stuff."

"Did you like it?"

"I did."

Kiki regarded him a moment. "So what made you leave it?" she asked. "You were on the east coast for a lot of years. Surely you had a life back there, friends and stuff. What made you come back to California?"

He stirred sugar into his iced tea. "Oh, a lot of things, I

guess," he said. "First of all, we don't have weather like this in D.C. in October. I missed the good weather."

She smiled faintly, sensing that it was something of an evasive answer. "I'm sorry," she said. "I shouldn't have asked such a personal question. I didn't mean to sound nosy."

He waved her off. "It wasn't a personal question at all," he said. "It's just a complicated answer. I guess the simplest explanation is that I was married for eighteen years but we divorced a few years ago and my son is grown up, living in Chicago. So, not really having any family left in D.C., I came home a year ago to help my dad with the family business."

"My dad told me that your brothers work for the business, too."

"They do."

"As much as I love my brother and sister, I'm not sure I could work with them. I think we'd all kill each other in the end."

He gave her a half-grin. "They don't step on my toes and I don't step on theirs."

"It must be different from what you were doing all those years with the CIA. It's like starting a new career all over again."

He shrugged. "I was working with my dad back in high school, so it's not completely new," he replied. "I'm the Vice President of Construction, Jesse is the V.P. of Operations, and Shaun is the CFO. It actually works out really well."

"Is your dad getting close to retiring?"

He nodded. "Probably in the next year or so, so he's leaving the business to us." He took a long drink of his iced tea. "And what about you? Did you work with your husband or have your own outside thing?"

She shook her head. "I've spent the past nineteen years raising kids and doing volunteer work," she replied. "I was a doctor's wife so I didn't have to work. Mark preferred that I didn't. He liked me to be the typical Orange County housewife, shuttling the girls around to soccer and dance, or volunteering with local organizations. I did a heck of a lot of volunteering, mostly with the girls' school or with the children's hospital charity. But my favorite thing was working with the California Symphony group out of Orange County. I did all of their fundraising for the arts, which benefited the local schools. I loved that."

"You don't do it anymore?"

"No."

"Why not?"

She shrugged, her bubbly personality dimming somewhat. "When Mark died, it's like I just kind of lost my drive. I tried to continue, but I was working with people who knew Mark and knew me, and every time I got together with them, it was like going to Mark's funeral again because all of those people had been there. I guess it sounds dumb, but I just couldn't look at their faces anymore. I wanted to come home, so here I am."

Trace could see that discussing her deceased husband

was a sore subject, making a mental note to veer away from that line of conversation in the future.

"Well, lucky for us you came back," he said quietly, his eyes glimmering warmly at her. "Your mom and dad must be happy about it."

Kiki nodded, forcing aside thoughts of Mark Conrad and her life that was. "Thrilled," she said. "But it's strange, you know? With the girls no longer living with me, and now I'm in a new house and all, I feel like I'm embarking on a new life. I've got a million family and friends all around me, but I just feel so alone moving forward. Kind of an exaggerated empty-nest syndrome."

He wasn't grinning anymore. His gaze was steady on her, appraising even. "You're not alone," he said quietly. "I felt the same way when I divorced and Alex went off to school. I swear I'd never felt more alone, like I had nothing to look forward to in life. But it's just not true. You've got that big ol' house and we'll get it all fixed up so you can open that venue."

Her smile was back. "I haven't given you the job, yet."

He grinned in return. "True enough. But even if you don't award us the bid, I'll still help you if you need it."

It was a very sweet declaration and Kiki sensed something more than normal friendliness. She was thrilled as well as terrified, but then she started thinking that she was just reading too much into it. Maybe it was just wishful thinking on her part. More than that, she was afraid to tell him that even with the new bid, she wouldn't be able to afford it. She knew that the moment she had looked at it.

She was sure the minute she told him, he would get into his truck and never look back. Selfishly, she just wanted to enjoy the man's company for a few more minutes before chasing him away. She lifted her glass to him as if to toast him.

"What are old friends for, eh?"

He clanked his iced tea glass against hers. "To renewing old friendships. And I'm sorry I didn't pay more attention to you back in high school."

She spent the next hour demanding to know what he meant by that. He spent the next hour refusing to answer.

He didn't want to call her.

That wasn't entirely true. He really *did* want to call her only he didn't want her to think he was harassing her about the job bid, or worse, stalking her. He'd already shown up once unannounced at her house. That was acceptable. But to do it twice might seem weird. So his only choice was to call her.

He never got the chance.

"Hey, son," Trace's dad stuck his head in his office. "I just got a call from Mrs. Conrad. She says she's going to put off doing anything to that house right now."

Trace looked at his father, shocked. "That place needs it badly," he said. "Did she say why?"

"No." His father shook his head. "I told her we'd hold the price for ninety days, though. Didn't you go out and see her yesterday?"

Trace stood up from behind his desk. "I did," he said. "In fact, I spent a couple of hours out there. She seemed on board with the new bid."

Rick Rocklin leaned against the doorjamb to his son's office. A handsome man in his seventies, he had the weather-worn skin and rough hands of a man who'd spent the majority of his life doing manual labor. He was also extremely sharp and business-savvy. He scratched his chin as he thought on his reply.

"Look," he said, lowering his voice. "I spoke with her dad when I went out to do the original estimate. He said that after Mrs. Conrad's husband died, they found out all sorts of things about the man, financial stuff if you know what I mean. I guess he left his wife and girls without much financial support, which is why I really tried to pare down the bid. I think you probably noticed how low it was."

Trace was feeling a good deal of pity along with his surprise. "I thought you'd lost your mind," he admitted. "Then I got a hold of it and shaved it down even more. Now...well, now it makes sense why you did what you did and why she looked kind of sick when I gave her the second bid. You know what I think?"

"What?"

"I think she had no idea what she was getting in to with that house and now that she's in too deep, she's stuck."

Rick wriggled his eyebrows and pushed himself off the doorjamb. "Probably," he sighed sadly as he turned away.

"But we don't work for free. It's too bad she's gotten herself into such a mess."

Trace watched his dad walk down the corridor of their fifteen thousand square foot office space, heading for his office. He was lost in thought, mulling over Kiki Conrad and her situation. Then he picked up his keys, got into his truck, and headed out for Pasadena.

Trace pulled up where he normally did in front of Kiki's house. It still looked the same, the big, old, haunted house that the kids in the neighborhood were afraid of. He climbed out of the truck as fast as he had turned it off, not even knowing what he was going to say to Kiki when he saw her. There were so many thoughts rolling through his head that it was difficult to isolate just one. But he knew one thing for certain; it had nothing to do with losing the bid. It had nothing to do with the money.

It had everything to do with her.

He opened the old wrought iron gate, listening to it creak. He was sure she could hear it, too, wherever she was, tipping her off that someone was approaching. Quietly, he made his way toward the house with the massive fountain a blockade between him and the front door. The fountain that was so precious to her.

As he approached the fountain, he could hear movement off to his right. Looking over, he could see Kiki buried up to her neck in old bushes and weeds. She was furiously pulling them out, tossing the dead old brush into great big piles. As he looked around, he could see that she had done quite a bit in the yard since yesterday. Her back was to him and he watched her for a few moments, thinking of the greeting he would deliver, when he caught movement at his feet. Looking down, he saw two big black doggy eyes gazing up at him.

"Hi, Bullfrog," he said, crouching down to pet the dog's head. "How long has your mom been at this?"

He said it loud enough for her to hear him. Catching wind of his voice, Kiki came to an unsteady halt and turned around with some shock. Trace smiled faintly when their eyes met.

"Hi," he said, trying to sound utterly casual. "I was just in the neighborhood and thought I'd drop by. Are you planning on ripping out this entire yard today?"

She wiped her gloved hand across her sweaty forehead, looking around at the mess she had created. "Probably not," she said. "It's a damn big yard. It's going to take me a while."

He gave the dog a final pat and stood up. "It's almost noon," he said. "I came to see if my lunch buddy wanted to grab some lunch."

She held his gaze a moment, perhaps with a great deal of regret, before lowering it and climbing her way out of the bushes. Her movements were slow and lethargic, like a kid facing something he didn't want to do. Once free of the bramble, she pulled her gloves off, slowly and pensively. She seemed unable to meet his gaze.

"I called your office earlier and spoke with your dad,"

she said softly, finally looking up at him. "Didn't he tell you?"

"Tell me what?"

She sighed heavily and lowered her gaze again. "Well..," she started hesitantly. "The house...it seems that I just can't do anything to it right now. You worked so hard on the bid and I appreciate it so much, but it's still way more than I can afford."

"So why did you have to call my dad and tell him? Why couldn't you tell me to my face?"

Her head snapped up to him. "Because...because I felt so bad about it. You worked so hard. I admit it—I was a coward to talk to your dad. It was just easier than disappointing you."

He cocked an eyebrow. "I'm just disappointed that you didn't think you could tell me personally. I thought we had a better relationship than that."

She shook her head and backed away from him, pulling off the hat and setting it down. When she looked at him with her flushed cheeks and sweetly mussed hair, there was a great deal of longing in her expression.

"Trace," she said softly. "You've been incredibly sweet and generous since we met, but don't think that you have to stroke me anymore. I promise, I'll give you the job as soon as I can afford it so you don't have to wine and dine me anymore."

He just looked at her. Then, his eyebrows lifted. "Is *that* what you think?" he asked, incredulous. "That I took you out to lunch to kiss up to you so I'd get the job?"

She shrugged lamely before finally nodding her head. "It's okay," she said. "I didn't mind. It was fun to catch up with you."

His jaw dropped. Then it closed again and he put his hands on his hips, facing her rather angrily. "Let me tell you something," he said. "I don't 'wine and dine' people to get a job. I never have and I never will. I took you out to lunch because I wanted to, plain and simple, and it has nothing to do with this goddamn job. Don't you get it? You've been all I can think about since the day we met. It's you...not the house, not the job. It's *you*."

Now it was her turn to stare at him with her mouth open. "W-What?" she stammered.

He could see how off guard she was and his manner softened. "I know it's crazy," he said softly. "I can't even explain it. All I know is that the past two days of knowing you are like nothing I've ever experienced. You have such life in you, Katharine. I can just feel it in everything about you and that's a really attractive quality. Don't you have any idea how beautiful you are?"

She closed her mouth but she took another step back from him, her eyes wide with surprise. "My...my name is Kiki."

"Kiki is a name for a kid and you're definitely not a kid," he said. "Katharine is a name for an incredibly beautiful woman, which you are."

"I...I don't even know what to say."

He shook his head. "You don't have to say anything," he said. "I'm not looking for an answer. But I have to be honest and tell you that I was kind of hoping we didn't get the job because it'll be a lot easier to date you if I'm not working for you. That would just make it awkward."

He didn't think her eyes could get any bigger. "Date me?"

"I'd like to."

"*Date* me?"

"Are you hard of hearing?"

She laughed, a reflexive reaction. Then, she burst into tears. Before Trace could say anything more, she ran into the house and slammed the door, leaving Trace and Stanley standing where she had left them.

Trace was looking at the closed door, hands still on his hips, wondering if he had just said something terribly wrong. He couldn't explain her reaction any other way and with that realization, he began to feel sick to his stomach. Maybe it had been too fast, too soon. He had never had a good sense of timing, anyway, or much tact. He was more of a straight-to-the-point person. God, he felt awful. Then he looked down at the dog, sitting patiently next to him.

He had an idea.

Kiki was still sobbing, sitting in her broken-down kitchen and trying to get a hold of herself. Trace's words had stunned her so much that she couldn't react any other way. He was perfect and wonderful, and she realized she wanted nothing more than to explore some manner of relationship with him. The past two days, getting to know him, having him around, had been heavenly. She could get used to it and the thought scared her to death. The last man she had around the house had died, leaving her to pick up the pieces. She wasn't sure she was ready to open herself up like that again.

As she sat there and wept, the back door to the utility porch creaked open. Startled, she froze, waiting for a person, maybe a burglar, to come strolling in, but instead, Stanley came trotting into the house. As he drew close, she saw something tied around his neck.

Climbing off the stool, she could see that a piece of paper was tied to his collar. Sniffling, curious, she untied the paper and unfolded it. It was an 8 ½ by 11 sheet of paper torn off from a yellow writing pad with a note of neat handwriting written in blue pen.

Dear Mom—
I've been asked by Mr. Rocklin to broker a peace treaty between you and him. Just so you know, he likes you a lot and he didn't mean to make you cry. He just wanted to tell you his thoughts. This is just my opinion, but maybe you should go out with him. I think he's a good guy and would be very nice to you. If you want to talk to him, he's outside on the porch. He says he's not going anywhere.

Love,
Bullfrog (Stanley)

P.S. I'm not doing this for free. If I can get you to come outside, he has to buy me Milkbone for a whole year.
P.S.S. I really like Milkbone.

Kiki read the note twice, giggling her way through it. It was clever and sweet, and her heart softened. But Trace didn't know the half of her situation and she was afraid to tell him, afraid it would change his opinion about her. Two days ago, she was pretty much alone in her new life, her new project, but forty-eight hours had seen a drastic change in the form of Trace Rocklin.

Sure, when she'd first seen him in her yard, she had made a mental joke about locking the gate so he couldn't escape. Never in her wildest dreams did she imagine he would respond or, better yet, come on to her. She still couldn't believe it.

Maybe that was her problem.

Torn, confused, and a little apprehensive, she looked around for a piece of paper but couldn't find one, so she ripped out a page of the pocket calendar in her purse and found a pen clipped in her wallet. Giving a lot of thought to the message she would respond with, she began to write.

Trace was sitting on the porch of the old house in an old folding chair that had probably been left by the previous occupants, watching the cars in the intersection beyond, wondering how Kiki had responded to his note. It *had* been rather clever of him, he thought. He wasn't even concerned with the fact that he had a lot of work waiting for him back at the office or the fact that his dad was probably beginning to wonder where he was. He was only thinking about Kiki and at least getting her to talk to him again. He was becoming increasingly concerned that he had frightened her off. As the minutes ticked by and the afternoon deepened, he was forced to admit that was a real possibility.

At nearly two in the afternoon, the enormous front door creaked open. Jolted with the sound and the thought of the only person who could have opened that door, he managed to keep his cool and continue staring out into the yard and street beyond. He didn't even turn to look to see if Kiki was standing there. He figured that if she wanted to talk to him, she would come out and make the first move.

So, he waited.

Seconds passed but nothing happened. Then something brushed up against his leg and he looked down to see the dog milling around by his feet. The first thing he noticed was a small, white piece of paper tied to the dog's collar. He reached down and plucked it out, unrolling the small, white note.

Dear Mr. Rocklin;
My mom says to tell you that she's sorry she ran away like a big baby. She just wasn't expecting what you said and it surprised her. My mom has been through a lot over the past year so she tends to get emotional about things. But she wants you to know that she's very flattered and she likes you, too.

Regards,
Stanley

P.S. I really hate being called Bullfrog. Really.

Trace just grinned. He read the note about a half dozen times before pulling a pen out of his pocket, turning the note over, and writing on the flip side. Five minutes later, the front door creaked open and Stanley got shoved in. The door silently closed behind him.

The dog, weary of being a pawn in his mom's potential romance, wandered upstairs without being seen and fell asleep on Kiki's bed.

She found the dog around sundown.

SIX

THE FRONT DOOR slowly creaked open, inviting the colors of sunset into the entry of the old home as it had done for a hundred years. Golds and yellows caressed the old wood floors of the parlor as the door opened wide. After a moment, a figure stepped through, onto the porch.

Trace was still sitting there. Kiki saw him, leaning back against the wall of the house near one of the windows. The shadows partially obscured him and the old chair he was planted in. He was just sitting there, staring off into the yard, as she made her way toward him.

Trace heard the door open but he didn't look over. In fact, he didn't look over until she was nearly upon him and, even then, it was because a glass of red wine suddenly appeared in front of his face. He looked at it before his gaze moved up to her face, so lovely in the dim sunset colors. His eyes locked with hers as he reached up, slowly, and took the wine she was extending to him. His fingers brushed against hers.

"Stanley didn't deliver your message in a timely manner," she said, taking the second and only other old metal chair on the porch, the one with only half a seat because the wood had broken off. "Apparently, all of this note delivery exhausted him and he went up to my bed to sleep it off. I just found him. I thought you'd gone home hours ago."

Trace didn't say a word. He stood up, took her by the wrist and pulled her up from the broken chair. He then sat her down on the chair that didn't have any sharp edges on the seat.

He perched on the end of the busted chair.

"I told Bullfrog to tell you that I wasn't leaving until you came out here to talk to me," he said simply.

"So you sat here for six hours?"

"Six hours, eight minutes, and twenty-nine seconds."

"You kept track?"

"I did."

Kiki clucked softly, incredulous. "Trace," she murmured, gently scolding. "You should have knocked on the door or something. I didn't even know you were still out here."

"Now you know."

Her eyes glittered at him warmly in response as she digested the information. She could hardly believe it, but it was just as sweet and flattering as it could be. Then she sipped at her wine, gazing off across the yard with the fountain in the middle of it. Her gaze grew distant.

"I guess you deserve something of an explanation," she said softly. "You opened yourself up to me so I guess it's only right you know what you opened yourself up *to*, if you know what I mean. Now, I'm going to preface this by saying I'm not looking for sympathy or pity. The situation is what it is and I'm perfectly capable of handling it. So don't get any funny ideas like I'm looking for a shoulder to cry on. I don't need one."

"Okay."

He said it rather resolutely so she continued. "Mark and I had a good marriage, or at least I thought it was good," she said. "We had our routine. I wasn't deliriously happy, but I wasn't unhappy, either. It was just the way our life was and I was satisfied. So you can imagine what a shock it was when he dropped dead of a heart attack at the age of fifty when he'd never had heart problems in his life. It was Christmastime last year when he went to work one morning and at noon, I got a call from his office manager; they were rushing Mark to the hospital because he was complaining about chest pains and by the time I got there, he had already passed. It was that fast."

By this time, Trace was looking at her with some sympathy, the precise thing she told him she didn't need from him. But he took a chance. "I'm sorry for you," he said quietly. "I really am."

She nodded and took another sip of wine. "I was sorry

for me, too," she said. "At the funeral, I was kind of in a daze. I remember so many people coming to pay respects, including this guy I'd never seen before. He kept calling Mark 'Patrick' when referring to him, so much so that my dad finally asked him if he was at the right funeral. The man assured him that he was but that, to him, Mark had always been known as 'Patrick'. I didn't give it much thought until it came time to settle his will and estate. Then, it started getting weird—it turned out that Mark had a life insurance policy but the beneficiaries were the girls and some guy named Robert Graves. When we looked into his will, the girls and I received a very small portion of his estate and the rest went to this guy, again, Robert Graves. My lawyer started looking into everything Mark had and all of it was signed over to this guy I'd never even heard of. When I contested the will, this guy, Robert, and his lawyer showed up to court. Turns out it was the guy at the funeral who had called him 'Patrick'. It would seem my perfect husband was leading a double life as a gay man and didn't want to 'come out' because of what it would do to his reputation and practice."

Trace was staring at her, feeling a good deal of disgust and sorrow on her behalf. "So what happened?"

She shrugged, taking another sip of her wine. "It turns out that Robert was really a very nice guy," she said. "He and Mark had been together eight years."

Trace's eyebrows lifted. "*Eight* years?" he repeated, trying not to sound too shocked. "And you never knew about him?"

Kiki shook her head, struggling not to appear too much

of an idiot. "He was a colleague of Mark's," she said softly. "Thinking back, I had seen him around and knew he worked with Mark, but I would have never suspected in a million years what was going on. Maybe that's phenomenally stupid of me, but it never occurred to me to suspect that my husband was having an affair with another man. If he goes to a convention with him, so what? If he goes to the movies with him, so what? I'm not thinking there's anything sexual. It never crossed my mind. But I suppose, in hindsight, maybe it should have. Mark was a very handsome and manly man, but our sex life was pretty nonexistent. It got worse over the years. He always had excuses, like he was too tired, or hurt himself working out, or things like that. It bothered me but he was a pretty great guy other than that, so I just let it slide. It never occurred to me he just wasn't interested in a woman sexually."

Trace wasn't sure what to say to all of that. After a moment, he simply shook his head. "Wow," he breathed. "So what happened with the will?"

She sighed faintly, thinking back on a time in her life that had been both shocking and disorienting.

"My lawyer said that Mark's will was air-tight," she said. "Here's the kicker—Mark and I were joint owners of our house, but Mark left his half to Robert, so I couldn't even sell the house without his consent. More than that, he got half of whatever the profits were. So I sat down with Robert one night and told him that the girls and I somehow needed to live, and that what Mark did to us wasn't fair. I couldn't do anything about the fact that he was a gay man so I wasn't going to let it bother me. What bothered me was that he used our marriage as his cover rather than be honest about it. I could have dealt with it better, I think. He should have just divorced me because it would have been easier for us both. Robert agreed with me and Quit-Claimed his portion of the house over to me so I could at least sell it and keep the money, which was very kind of him. He's even contributed to the girls' college funds and returned the money from our joint savings account. I know it sounds really weird that my husband's gay lover has been so kind to me, but I'm thankful for small things, I suppose. He's actually become a friend."

Trace's brow furrowed. "The man had an affair with your husband and he's become your friend?"

Kiki sighed, turning her gaze to him. "I told you it's weird," she said simply. "I meant it. Robert is a very kind man. It's not his fault that he fell in love with Mark, or vice versa. I just wish they'd been honest about it."

Trace mulled her statement over, thinking that she was an extraordinarily forgiving woman. Either that, or an emotional cripple looking for any port in the storm, but she really didn't seem to be the type. In fact, she seemed very normal and settled about the whole thing. He admired that kind of attitude.

"You're extremely magnanimous," he said after a moment. "I'm not sure I could be so forgiving."

She shrugged, averting her gaze. "Anger and bitterness are such destructive emotions," she murmured. "I admit I was a basket case when I first found out. Who wouldn't be?

But I don't want any destructive or crippling emotions in my life, so I've had to forgive in order to move on. And if my husband's gay lover wants to contribute to my children's college, then I'm going to let him. For my girls' sake, I'm damn well going to let him."

Trace liked the backbone he was seeing in her. The woman had been dealt a hell of a hand in life. He was coming to appreciate her fortitude very much.

"More power to you," he lifted his wine glass to her. "You're doing what you have to do."

"You'd better believe it," she agreed, "which brings me to this house. I told you before I wanted to come home to my roots to start fresh. This house symbolized that. After selling the house in Orange County and purchasing this one, I only have eighty thousand dollars set aside to restore it. That's it. Remember I asked you what was absolutely necessary?"

"I do."

"I just don't have the money for anything more. But I need to get this place, at least, somewhat habitable so I can start generating some income to finish it off."

Trace sighed, pondering her dilemma, before taking another sip of wine. He just sat there, watching the dusk descend over the trees, watching the yard grow dark. He had a lot of thoughts on the matter and suspected, at some point, he'd better let her in on what he was thinking. But he wanted to do it in a way that wasn't going to make her run crying back into the house again.

"Can we talk about it over dinner?" he finally asked. "I'm getting kind of hungry."

She sighed. "Trace, I want to be really clear about this," she said softly. "If you work on my house, I won't date you. I can't. I don't want you to think I'm sleeping with you just to get free work out of you and, coming to suspect you are a kind and generous man, you might want to restore much more than what I'm paying for. It just wouldn't be right. So it's either the house or me."

He looked at her. "That's my choice?"

She nodded. "As hard as it is for me to say that, that's about the gist of it right now."

He cleared his throat softly and stood up from the broken chair, setting his empty wine glass down on an equally broken-down matching table nearby. Shoving his hands in his pockets, he casually strolled to the edge of the porch, his gaze moving out over the yard. It took him a moment to realize that Stanley had followed him, now sitting patiently next to his feet. He looked down at the dog.

"Help me out here, Bullfrog," he muttered. "You said you'd be my wingman. What do I do?"

Sitting back in the shadows, Kiki couldn't help but grin as Trace had a one-sided conversation with the dog. He looked down at the mutt, nodding his head as if the dog were telepathically speaking to him, before turning around to look at her.

"Can I make a counter-proposal?" he asked.

Kiki shrugged. "I'm listening."

He paused a moment, thoughtfully, before speaking. "If you and I date, it's going to be exclusive because I don't play the field, I'm not a 'dater', and I don't share. Even if we eventually decide to part as friends, for the time being and while we're getting to know each other, I won't see anyone else and I don't want you to, either. Okay?"

She conceded the point. "Agreed," she replied. "Is that your proposal?"

He shook his head. "No," he said. "People who date exclusively are usually called boyfriend and girlfriend."

She fought off a smile. "That's true."

"So, as your boyfriend, I'm perfectly free to work on this house anytime, anyway, because you belong to me so, in a sense, the house does as well. Are you with me so far?"

Her mouth turned into a dubious frown. "Now, wait a minute. I just said that...."

"Okay, so if you won't go for that, go for this," he said, cutting her off. "You need to generate income from this place, right?"

"Right."

"You want to open it as a bed and breakfast and micro-wedding venue, right?"

"Right."

"Would you consider a boarder, instead? At least temporarily?"

Her eyes widened with surprise. "A tenant?" she repeated. "I...I hadn't really thought about it."

He began to make his way in her direction. "Think about it," he said. "I'll rent a room here but instead of paying you rent, I'll fix up the house to earn my keep. How does that sound?"

She was on her feet. "You're crazy," she exclaimed, but it was without force. "You'd rent a room from me but..?

He held up a finger, cutting her off. "You gave me a choice about five minutes ago—the house or you," he said firmly. "Now, I'm giving *you* a choice—I work on the house as your boyfriend or as your boarder. You decide."

She crossed her arms, cocking an eyebrow at him. "I *have* decided. I've decided you're crazy."

His lips twitched with a smile and he came closer to her, closer than he ever had. Kiki stood her ground as he brushed up against her, his warm and powerful body sending shockwaves of excitement coursing through her limbs. Having him so close, but not being held by him, was the most painful and exhilarating sensation she'd ever known. He just stood there, his torso against hers, his muscular arms hanging at his sides, gazing down at her with a sultry half-grin on his face.

She began to tremble. She couldn't control it because having him so close, so magnetically close, was like torture. She knew he could see the lust and longing in her expression and he surely could see that her lips were trembling, but he did nothing more than dip his head and kiss her softly on the cheek. It was warm, gentle, and utterly sexy. Kiki nearly collapsed.

"Maybe I am," he whispered. "You've got until tomorrow morning to decide. Go back in the house now and lock the door. I'm going to stand here until you do. And then I'll be back in the morning for your answer."

Kiki was having trouble breathing and the quivering of her body had grown worse. All she wanted to do was throw her arms around him and feel his lips against hers. Nothing in her life had ever called so strongly to her. But she somehow managed to stumble away from him, her mind so much mud, calling to Stanley as she went. The dog trotted into the house after her and she began to close the door, her eyes on Trace standing over by the porch steps. He smiled at her.

"Close the door," he commanded softly. "I'll be back in the morning and you'd better have the right answer for me."

Kiki closed the door and threw the big, old, iron bolt. She stood there for the longest time, indecisive and somewhat overwhelmed.

Then she just grinned.

Trace was on his way home when the phone rang. Glancing at the number, he grinned as he answered it.

"Go for Rocklin," he said.

The voice on the other end snorted. "Christ," the man muttered. "You just took me back several years to a time I still have nightmares about."

Trace chuckled. "Nostalgic, eh?"

"Stop answering your damn phone like that, Trace."

Trace continued to laugh. "Suck it up, buttercup," he said. "How the hell are you, Beau?"

On the other end of the line, Beau Meade started to laugh because Trace was. "You really are a piece of work," he said. "Don't make me sorry that I've called you."

The laughter faded, but Trace was still grinning. "You'd never feel that way," he said. "What has you calling California at this hour?"

On the other end of the line, Beau yawned. "What time is it?" he said. He clearly glanced at his watch because he grunted. "Oh, I see. Well, it's not too late. Why? Are you busy?"

"Just heading home," he said. "How are things down Mississippi way for the sheriff of Tallahassee County?"

He was referring to the fact that Beau had been elected county sheriff quite some time ago. In fact, Trace had been present at the election in support of his friend and had been with Beau to celebrate the win. He couldn't have been prouder of the man had he been his own brother.

"The usual," Beau said. Then, he paused. "Actually, that's not entirely true."

"Oh?" Trace said. "Why? What's up?"

Beau seemed hesitant. "There are just some things I can't talk to my friends about round here," he said. "Everybody knows everybody. You know how small towns are. And I honestly don't trust any of my friends not to talk, but you don't have any skin in the game, so you won't talk."

"About what?"

"I met someone."

That perked Trace up. He was just getting on the 210 Freeway, heading east, and almost missed the on-ramp because of what Beau said.

"You?" he said, finally merging into traffic. "I don't believe it."

"Believe it."

"Who is she?"

Beau snorted. "That's the funny part," he said. "She's from California. She works for a law firm in Los Angeles."

"Nice," Trace said. "What's she doing in rural Mississippi?"

"Her grandmother just died," he said. "Remember when you visited a few years ago? Remember I drove you around and showed you the historic district of Pea Ridge?"

"I do," Trace said. "Gorgeous old homes. Speaking of gorgeous old homes..."

"What about it?"

"Forget it," Trace said. "I'll tell you after we talk about you. What about the historic district?"

"That's where her grandmother's house is," Beau said. "The biggest, baddest one of the bunch. They call it Glory."

Trace shrugged. "I probably saw it if you showed it to me, but I don't remember it," he said. "What about it?"

"Nothing, really," Beau said. "Except it's got a hell of a history. Turns out her great-grandfather was the nastiest son-of-a-bitch the town has ever seen. I mean, this guy was a piece of work, Trace. Ran the town like his own private empire. Killed people. Destroyed the lives of others. You name it, Laveau Hembree did it. The older folks in this town still won't talk about him, like they're afraid he'll rise up out of his grave and come for them. He's bad news."

"Wow," Trace said. "Sounds like a hell of a guy."

"You're not kidding," Beau said. "Anyway, his great-granddaughter—Lucy—is someone I just met a few days ago, but I'm telling you that she's something special. I feel like...like I could live the rest of my life with her and be pretty happy about it, to be honest. But the fact that her great-grandfather is who he was..."

"It's giving you second thoughts?"

"Maybe," Beau said. "And I didn't tell you the best part—my grandfather was on this guy's payroll."

"Wasn't he the police chief or something?"

"He sure was."

"So what are you telling me?" Trace asked. "Are you looking for my opinion on this? What I think about it?"

"Yeah, maybe," Beau said. "Lucy and I haven't done anything but talk, but there's something there, Trace. A spark. I haven't felt that kind of attraction in years. Maybe I just need a perspective that's not from this town and doesn't know the history of the Meade and Hembree families."

"What kind of perspective?"

"I don't really know," Beau said. "I suppose...do I get mixed up in something that might cost me votes when I run for Sheriff again? I know that sounds stupid, but it's been so long since I've been in a relationship...and you know how badly Debra burned me...that I don't trust my own judgment."

It was a heavy conversation and an unexpected one, but Trace took it seriously. Debra Meade, Beau's wife, had left him after their third child was born. She simply decided she didn't want to be a wife and mother any longer, leaving Beau with three young kids and an upended life. That had been after he'd quit the CIA to be a regular father and husband, so Debra's decision had been a blow. But he'd survived—Beau was most definitely a survivor—and he was one of the most level-headed guys Trace knew, so if he was asking questions about a woman—and old family prejudices in the South—then it must be serious, indeed.

"Well," Trace said thoughtfully. "I can't tell you what to do, but if it were me...and this woman made me feel all lit up like this woman evidently does to you...I wouldn't worry about old prejudices. That's just the old generation, Beau. I'll bet the middle-aged and voting-aged people don't give a shit. And you have to do what makes you happy. You've gone too long not being happy, so it's your time."

On the other end of the line, Beau sighed faintly. "That's exactly what I was thinking," he said. "But, like I said, I just don't trust my judgment anymore. I'm glad to see it's still intact."

"Still, buddy. Don't worry so much."

"Thanks," Beau said, sounding relieved. "Well, I don't want to keep you. I know you're a busy guy. How's civilian life treating you?"

Trace grinned. "After two years of it?" he said. "Better. I like being home. I like spending time with my dad and brothers. I don't miss the...well, let's just say I don't miss it."

"I'll bet," Beau said. "I'm sorry the way it ended for you, though. With Marcos and all. Sometimes life doesn't go as planned."

That was true, but it was something Trace didn't want to discuss. Not even with Beau. Leaving the CIA hadn't been a choice for Trace as much as it had been a necessity. If he hadn't, he probably would have ended up in an asylum. That one, last critical mission that had cost him more than the loss of a colleague. It had cost him his loyalty to his job, his country, his everything. It had cost him his confidence and two years later, he still didn't want to think about it or talk about it.

"No, it sure doesn't," he finally said, noticing that his off-ramp for home was coming up. "In fact, speaking of life not going as planned, you're not the only one with some lady-news."

"Really?" Beau said, sounding very interested. "You've met someone, too?"

Trace's thoughts drifted to the goddess with the beautiful eyes and smash-face dog. "Believe it or not, a girl I used to know in high school," he said. "We've just reconnected and that's all I can tell you for now. It's still very new. But much like you, I feel...encouraged. Really encouraged."

"Wow," Beau said. "That says a lot coming from you. I'm happy for you, Trace, truly."

"Thanks," Trace said. "I'll tell you more when I know more. There just isn't a lot to say about it right now."

"Same," Beau said. "Hey, it was good talking to you. Thanks for lending an ear."

"You're welcome," Trace said. "Maybe I'll fly out to Mississippi one of these days or we can meet in Memphis or Nashville or something. Eat some good barbeque."

"You name the weekend and I'll be there."

"Reed, too?"

"He'd kill us if we ate barbeque without him."

Trace snorted. "I get it," he said. "What about the rest of the team?"

"Another time."

"Agreed. Talk to you later."

"Take care."

Trace hung up the phone, smiling as he rolled the conversation over in his mind. So Beau had found some-one, had he? Trace was genuinely happy for him. But, truth be told, he was happier for himself.

He'd definitely found someone, too.

Maybe permanently.

SEVEN

SHE HEARD THE GLASS BREAKING.

At first, Kiki thought she had been dreaming. In her dark bedroom on the second floor, she glanced over at the clock. *4:01 a.m.* Rolling over, she glanced at Stanley, who was lying in his fluffy little bed next to the wall. The dog was awake, his head up and his ears alert. Kiki lay there a moment in silence, listening for any further sounds, when she heard more glass breaking and a big bang. Stanley leapt to his feet and began barking savagely.

Frightened, Kiki slithered out of bed and grabbed the golf club that she kept under her bed for protection. It was silly, really, and she had been telling herself that she would go to the gun shop and buy a small handgun for protection, but she just hadn't made the trip yet. Now she was wishing she had.

Scooting to her bedroom door, she cracked it open. She couldn't see any movement but she could definitely hear something downstairs. It sounded like footsteps, shuffling around. Closing the door, she rushed back to her nightstand and picked up her cell phone. She had to go through the operator to call the 911 system of the Pasadena Police Department, but they connected her right away. A very helpful dispatcher on the other end told her to stay put, lock the door, and stay on the phone until the police arrived. Taking her golf club and Stanley into the bathroom with her, she locked the door.

The noises were getting closer and she was nearing panic at that point. The intruders were definitely in the upper hall, heading for her bedroom. She could hear the floorboards creaking. As she tried to stay calm, listening to the dispatcher assure her that the cops were nearly there, she reached into one of the bathroom drawers and pulled out a very sharp pair of scissors. They were dangerous and a better weapon than the golf club. She put Stanley in the shower enclosure and shut it, standing flush against the wall next to the door with the scissors in one hand and her phone in the other.

The footsteps were in her room now. She heard them enter when the door creaked. Then someone tried the bathroom door and Stanley started barking like crazy. The bathroom door rattled violently and the old lock, weakened with age, began to give way when someone kicked it.

The dispatcher heard a lot of screaming after that and when the phone hit the old tile floor, the line went dead.

. . .

It was five thirty in the morning and Trace had already had two cups of coffee. He exited the 210 Freeway at Fair Oaks Avenue and headed north towards Kiki's house. He'd been up since four, inexplicably unable to sleep, and had waited an hour before showering and getting in his truck.

He stopped at a Starbucks once he got off the freeway and got two cups of coffee. A couple of miles up Fair Oaks was the turn for Kiki's house and he made the right-hand turn to the east. Her house was two blocks down on the corner and he could already see it, the big bastion set against the coming dawn. He could also see several police units and an ambulance parked all around it and, suddenly, his happy morning wasn't so happy. In fact, he was immediately concerned.

His heart leapt into his throat.

The coffee was forgotten as he came to a screeching halt across the street because her house was surrounded by rescue vehicles. Turning the truck off, he bailed out and ran across the fairly busy street without looking, dodging between two cop cars and charging through the old wrought iron gate, which was open. There were cops in the yard, on the porch, and other people he really didn't care about and couldn't make out in the darkness. The first cop he came across reached out and grabbed him.

"Hold on." The Black officer had a grip on his arm. "Who are you?"

Trace was fairly close to a state of panic. "I'm...the woman that lives here," he stammered. "I'm her... boyfriend. Is she okay? What happened?"

The cop didn't let him go. He put the radio micro-phone clipped to his collar up to his mouth. "What's your name, son?" he asked quietly.

"Rocklin. Trace Rocklin."

The officer contacted someone on the radio and gave them Trace's name. There was some chatter coming back, but Trace was ready to explode.

"Jesus Christ," he hissed. "Would you just tell me if she's okay? What happened?"

The cop let go of him and held up a soothing hand as he exchanged information with someone on the radio. Trace finally heard someone clear him to be there but he was directed to remain outside with an escort for the moment. The cop acknowledged the instructions before answering Trace.

"The paramedics are with her," he finally said.

Trace didn't know if he felt better or worse. "What in the hell happened?"

"Break in," the cop replied. "So...you don't live here with her?"

Trace shook his head. "No."

"It's just her?"

He nodded. "Yes."

The cop wriggled his eyebrows. "Hmmm," he said as he put his hands on his hips, a rather beefy man with a shaved head, and looked around the yard. "You know, I remember this house growing up. The neighborhood is a little better now than it was when I was a kid, but a woman living in this area alone...I don't know if I would be comfortable with that. The projects around the corner at Summit and Painter aren't the greatest. They're still pretty bad."

Trace couldn't disagree. "She bought the house to restore it," he explained, but he really didn't want to talk about the house. He wanted to talk about Kiki. "Can I see her, please?"

The cop shook his head patiently. "The detectives are still questioning her. You can when they're finished."

"Why are they questioning her?"

The cop scratched his chin, rather reluctantly. "The guy that broke into the house is dead," he said, somewhat quietly. "It's a clear case of self-defense, but the detectives still need to question her."

Trace's eyes widened. "Did she kill him?"

The cop nodded slowly. "Looks that way."

Trace couldn't help it. His jaw dropped. "Oh, my God," he breathed, trying to wrap his mind around the news. "Well, hell, does she at least have a lawyer with her while they question her? Why can't I go up there and at least sit with her while this is going on?"

The cop patted him on the shoulder to calm him down because he was getting agitated. "Hold on," he said as he spoke into his radio again and some chatter went back and forth. "I'm working on it."

Trace was agitated and upset, making it difficult for him to stand still. He shifted around on his big legs, his gaze moving over the yard, the porch, and all of the activity going on. There were cops in the bushes, on the porch, checking windows, and shining their flashlights on the ground as they looked for evidence. Then, a cop emerged from the front door carrying something in his arms. It took Trace a moment to realize the man had Stanley. He bolted for the dog before the Black cop could stop him.

"Bullfrog," he said, going straight for the dog with his arms out. "Can I please have the dog? Is he okay?"

The cop holding Stanley only handed him over when the Black cop nodded at him. Trace collected Stanley and scratched him on the head.

"Hey, buddy." He actually hugged the dog, glad to see him. "Are you okay?"

"He's fine." The cop who had brought the dog out of the house spoke. "He was in the shower enclosure the entire time. Not a scratch."

Trace looked at the tall, rather heavy-set White cop/dog-handler. "How's Katharine?" he wanted to know. "Can I please see her?"

"One of the detectives is going to talk to you in a minute."

Trace knew he had to be satisfied with that for the moment. At least he was getting somewhere. He stood there and held the dog, petting his head for a few minutes before finally setting him to his feet so he could go do his doggy business. He ended up following Stanley around the yard as the dog sniffed and dug around, being typically nosy. This went on for about twenty minutes until a handsome man in a pair of dark slacks and a dress shirt approached him from the house.

"Are you the boyfriend?" the man asked as he extended his hand to Trace, who took it. "I'm Detective Irwin."

Trace shook his hand and released it. "Trace Rocklin."

"Nice to meet you," Irwin said. "Mrs. Conrad wants to see you, but I wanted to talk to you first and explain what's going on."

Trace bent over and scooped the dog up before he could run off. "I'd appreciate it."

The detective motioned him to walk with him towards the house. "I take it you don't live here with her?"

Trace shook his head as he followed the detective. "Not yet," he replied. "We were, in fact, discussing that topic today."

Irwin nodded. "When was the last time you saw her?"

"Last night at about six."

"Do you have a house key?"

"No."

"Where do you live?"

"Monrovia. About ten miles east, near the mountains."

"And you were there all night?"

"I was."

"Any witnesses to that?"

"I saw one of my brothers at about ten when he swung by my house to pick up a tool chest I had. Why?"

The detective shook his head. "Just asking," he replied. "It's all routine, especially when there's a death involved."

Trace sighed heavily as they mounted the steps to the porch. "So what happened?"

The detective opened the enormous front door. "As far as we can tell, a single intruder broke in at around four in the morning," he said as they stepped into the cavernous sitting room, dimly lit by a single floor lamp. "He broke in through the utility room by smashing a window and climbing in. So he comes inside and makes it upstairs where Ms. Conrad is hiding in the master bathroom. The intruder hears her, kicks the door in to get to her, and she's waiting for him with a pair of scissors. A fight ensues and she manages to shove the scissors into his left eye, into his brain. Pretty much killed him instantly."

By this time, Trace was staring at him in horror. "Oh, God," he breathed. "Is she really okay? He didn't...rape her, did he?"

Irwin led him over to the stairs that went up to the second floor. He paused and faced Trace. "He didn't rape her," he muttered. "Look, we think the guy was a drug addict looking for money, or drugs, or whatever. He was probably high, which made him crazy, and he attacked your girlfriend. There's no question of that. She's terrified and banged up, and she's been throwing up pretty steadily since we arrived. We called the paramedics but she doesn't want to go with them. For her sake, she really should. The guy smacked her around pretty good. I agreed to let you come into the crime scene to see her in the hope that you could talk her in to going to the hospital."

Trace felt sick. He nodded, firmly, and followed the detective up the stairs and into the dark hallway on the second floor. There were more cops up there, plus fire department personnel. The hallway ended at the master bedroom and he entered the fairly crowded room, which included the body of the burglar still lying in the bathroom doorway. The Crime Scene Investigation team was there, photographing and cataloging everything.

The sight of the blood and body didn't bother him in the least because he'd seen much worse during his days with the CIA. *Much* worse. In fact, it hardly registered with him other than the man was white and young. His focus was on Kiki, sitting on the bed in full view of the death and blood.

The first thing he did was growl.

"Jesus," he said as he turned to the detective. "Does she really have to sit in here with this mess right in front of her? Couldn't you have at least moved her to another room for questioning?"

Kiki heard Trace's voice, turning to see him in the bedroom doorway holding Stanley in his arms, looking rather distressed. The tears that had so recently fled returned as their eyes met and her face crumpled. Tears poured down her cheeks. Trace went to her immediately, setting Stanley on the bed so he could put his arms around her.

The first feel of his arms around her, safe and strong and warm, did Kiki in. She sobbed deeply, her face in his shoulder, as he held her tightly. She was still terrified, disoriented and overwhelmed with everything that had happened. It was rather ironic that her first real embrace with Trace had to be over a crisis, but she didn't care. In fact, she was hugely grateful for it. She'd never felt more comfort, from anyone, in her life.

Trace was feeling much the same sensations. It was warm and wonderful and delicious to have her in his arms, but the circumstances were less that desirable. Regardless, he was thrilled, and he'd never felt more protective over anything in his life.

"Hey," he said as he kissed her head. "Let me get a look at you. They told me you got pretty banged up.'"

Sobbing, she wouldn't let him go when he tried to get a look at her injuries. She just wanted to be held, so Trace gave up trying to loosen her grip and just held her, rocking her gently as she cried. She caved into him and he held her snuggly, loving the feel of her against him in spite of the circumstances. He could have very easily lost himself in that embrace. But then he began to look around, seeing the paramedics watching what was going on. The guys had gloves on, and it was obvious they'd been trying to examine her. Given her mental state, Trace was pretty sure she hadn't made it easy. He was a bit firmer when he pulled back the second time.

"Hey," he said, gently but firmly. He cupped her face between his two big hands. "Let me have a look at you, okay? You're scaring me to death. Where did he hurt you?"

Kiki struggled to calm down, her sobs now reducing to hiccups. "I...I don't even know," she sniffled. "It all happened so fast."

He sighed sympathetically and kissed her forehead. "Did you let the paramedics look at you?"

She nodded, pale and watery-eyed. "Uh-huh."

He looked as if he didn't believe her. "Did you really."

Again, she nodded. "Well...I tried. I think I did. But I don't need to be looked at. I'm okay."

He looked up to the three men standing next to the bed, who looked back at him with various expressions of disbelief. Trace suspected what their expressions meant. He nodded his head in Kiki's direction.

"Go ahead," he told them softly. "Do what you need to do."

Kiki stiffened up but Trace put a big arm around her shoulders, calming her. "I won't leave, I promise," he said, trying to position himself so he was blocking her view of the corpse in the bathroom door. "I'll sit right here. Bullfrog and I would feel a lot better if you'd let the paramedics examine you. He's pretty shook up - look at him. He's all kinds of crazy. I think you need to let the paramedics look at you so he'll calm down."

That brought a weak smile to her lips as she glanced over at Stanley, who was now sleeping on the pillow behind her like he'd been on a three-day drinking binge. The dog was as far as he could be from being shook up. With Trace's calming presence, the paramedics were able to do a bit more than just take her blood pressure and give her a cursory exam. She gagged once during their exam, dry-heaving as a result of her nerves, and the paramedics were gentle with her about it. As they worked, Trace watched closely. He even helped them when they wanted to get a look at her right forearm but she wasn't too forthcoming in showing them. Detective Irwin stood by, taking notes.

"Are those marks on her forearm defensive wounds?" he asked the paramedic.

The older paramedic with the dark hair and blue eyes nodded. "Yes," he said clinically. "She's got them on her hands, too, and on her left forearm to a lesser degree."

Irwin jotted notes before looking at Kiki. "Do you remember much after he broke into the bathroom, Mrs. Conrad?" he asked, not unkindly. "Did he say anything? Did you immediately try to fight him off or did you first try to get away from him?"

Kiki was in a daze, watching them examine her right arm. "I'm not really sure," she sighed. "He kicked the door in and then everything seems like a blur after that. I had the scissors in my hand because it was the only weapon I had and I just started slashing at him when he came at me. He...he pushed me or hit me. I don't really know, but I fell on the floor and he started kicking me. So I stabbed his foot, I think. I remember hacking at his shoes. He started yelling and when he bent down, I slashed at his head."

"That must have been when you stabbed his eye," the detective said quietly. "He probably bent over as a reflex action when you stabbed his foot."

Kiki nodded, not really wanting to think about that moment in time. "I don't really know," she said. "All I know is that his head came down and I aimed for it. I knew if I didn't kill him, he was going to kill me."

She started to weep, softly, and Trace hugged her as he

looked up at the detective. He didn't want her getting all worked up again. "Are we done with this?" he asked softly. "I'd like to get her to the hospital."

Irwin nodded. "Actually, that's the most coherent thing we've gotten out of her since we arrived," he said. "We can stop for now but I'm going to want to talk to her again tomorrow, once she's had a chance to calm down and rest."

Trace nodded but he was already impatient, already wanting to get Kiki out of that room with the dead guy in it, a constant reminder of her brush with death.

"At least let her get some sleep," he said. Then he looked at the paramedics. "I'll help you get her downstairs."

The paramedics were already moving as Trace stood up, pulling Kiki up with him. She was trembling; he could feel it. Bending over, he picked her up and cradled her against his broad chest, but the moment he started to move, she balked.

"My dog," she said. "I don't want to leave him behind."

She was starting to get panicky. He gave her a squeeze. "Let me get you downstairs and then I'll come back for Bullfrog. I promise I won't leave him behind, okay?"

That seemed to calm her down and she nodded. He kissed her cheek and took her downstairs where the ambulance attendants and the gurney were waiting. Kiki eyed the gurney.

"Trace," she said softly. "I really don't think I need to go to the hospital. I didn't break anything. I just want to go to sleep."

He was gentle with her. "Honey, I'd feel much better if you'd just let the doctor check you out to make sure you're okay," he said, his voice low. "It scares the shit out of me to think of you fighting with that guy. He could have really hurt you. I just want to make sure you're okay. For my own peace of mind, will you *please* just go and get checked out?"

He turned it around a little, making it seem like she was doing him a favor by going to the hospital. She was reluctant, but agreed.

"Okay," she said as he set her to her feet. "But will you please come with me? I don't like hospitals."

"Of course I will," he said, rubbing her back soothingly as the paramedics coaxed her onto the gurney. "I'm going to go upstairs and get Bullfrog and meet you there, okay?"

"Okay."

He bent over and kissed her on the lips, the first real kiss between them. It was as soft, warm and sweet as it could possibly be, and he kissed her again just because he liked it so much. Then he winked at her.

"I'll meet you over there, I promise," he murmured. "But I've got to go get the dog before he starts tearing people up. He's so damn vicious."

She giggled. "Thank you for taking care of him."

"Anytime. He's my wingman, remember?"

She grinned as the paramedics got her situated and the ambulance attendants strapped her down. At least she was smiling, which he was thankful for. He continued to stand there and smile at her as they got her oriented and wheeled her out of the front of the house just as the coroner was entering. He thought it might set her off again but she didn't even look at the guys in white. She just lay there, head turned and eyes closed. When she was finally wheeled through the door and heading to the ambulance, Trace bolted up the stairs and back to the master bedroom where the investigation team was winding up their fact-finding mission. He went straight for Detective Irwin.

"I'm going to the hospital with her," he told the man, "but I need to fix the broken window downstairs and secure the house. Can I go ahead and do that?"

Irwin nodded. "Yes," he said. "I think we're pretty much finished here. It didn't take a brain surgeon to figure this all out, so give us a couple of hours and we should be finished."

Trace nodded, digging in his pocket and pulling out a business card. He handed it to the detective. "Call me when you're finished so I can start getting the place secure," he said. "I'd appreciate it."

Irwin looked at the card. "Rocklin Construction?" he snorted. "You guys did the new police wing."

"I know."

Irwin tucked the card into his pocket. "I'll call you when we're ready to move," he said. "But you might want to consider getting a cleaning company in here to take care of the blood on the floor. She's not going to want to come home to this."

"I'm way ahead of you on that."

The detective nodded and Trace went over to the bed

where Stanley was snoring. He was also farting up a storm. Trace wrinkled his nose at the stinky dog as he shook him awake before picking him up with one arm. With the other hand, he dug into his pocket for his cell phone.

He was making calls before he even left the house.

EIGHT

THE DAY dawned overcast and misty in cool contrast to the unseasonable warmth of the past few days. It was starting to feel like winter now, cool and wet, as the winter season descended. Before Trace reached the hospital, he hit a drugstore that opened up early and picked up a few things for the dog, namely food, bottled water, and a cushy, plush doggy bed that had been on sale. He even picked up a squeak toy. He wasn't sure how long he was going to be at the hospital and didn't want to leave the dog without food or water.

Pulling in the parking structure across from the emergency room of Huntington Memorial Hospital in Pasadena, he made sure the truck was near the guy taking the money for the parking fees. In the back seat of his crew cab, he set the dog up with kibble and water in his new, red, plastic, doggy bowl and put the bed and toy on the floor. He also spread out parts of the Wall Street Journal he had rolled up in the back seat, knowing it wasn't much of a barrier against doggy accidents but there wasn't much he could do about it.

Cracking the windows and locking the truck, he made sure to tell the guy at the ticket booth about the dog in the truck and gave the guy his business card in case Stanley started barking or howling. The guy seemed amiable enough and Trace hightailed it to the emergency room.

By the time he got there, Kiki had already been examined. She was bruised but had suffered no broken bones. When Trace arrived in the examining room, she was waiting for the nurse to bring her prescription painkillers and a release form. He sat next to the bed and held her hand, telling her about Stanley out in the truck with his new bed and toy, and he could see that the care he had taken with the dog pleased her immensely. He refrained from talking about the house, or anything else serious, as he tried to keep the conversation light.

In fact, Kiki seemed quiet and exhausted, and he didn't blame her in the least, so at some point he stopped talking and let her doze off, still holding her hand. He tried to move, once, but she awoke instantly and held on to him with a death grip, so he reassured her that he wasn't going anywhere and she drifted back off to sleep again. When the nurse returned, he caught the woman's attention.

"Why is she passed out like this?" he asked, concerned. "Are you sure she's okay?"

The nurse, a Black woman with beautiful eyes, set the

prescription bottles she was holding on the counter and began filling out the release forms.

"She's fine," she said. "The doctor gave her a shot of valium because she was pretty worked up when she got here. She needs to calm down and rest, so take her home after this and let her sleep."

Trace's gaze moved to Kiki, passed out on the gurney. He wasn't going to take her home, not by a long shot. At least not today. His focus moved back to the pill bottles on the counter.

"What are those for?" he asked.

The nurse picked up one of them. "Anaprox for any stiffness or aches she might have," she said, then looked at the other one. "This is Xanax in case she starts having anxiety issues. It'll calm her down quickly. And the last bottle is Ambien in case she has trouble sleeping."

He lifted his eyebrows at all of the drugs. When the nurse was finished with the paperwork, she turned to him as she was reading something in the paperwork package.

"Are you Mr. Rocklin?" she asked.

He nodded. "I am."

The nurse handed him a pen. "You can sign her out, then. I'll release her to you."

"What's my name doing in the paperwork?"

"She must have given it to the admitting nurse as an authorized person."

Satisfied with the answer, Trace signed Kiki out of the emergency room. He took her prescription pills and put them in his pocket. Finally, turning to Kiki, she was still dead asleep on the gurney. He stood there a moment, just looking at her, seeing the woman in a different light. Things were deeper with them now, away from the cursory levels of acquaintance, and getting down to the nitty-gritty of who, and what, a person was. He was coming to learn her character, her personality, and loving it. He hoped she thought the same of him. As he stood there gazing at her, the nurse spoke beside him.

"I'll bring you a wheelchair," she told him.

He waited until the woman brought the wheelchair into the exam room before trying to wake her. Kiki was extremely groggy as he helped her off the table and into the chair. He told the nurse he'd meet her at the entry with his truck and made his way back to the parking structure. The misty morning had turned into full-blown rain as he ran across the street and unlocked his truck.

Stanley had made himself at home on the back seat, chewing happily on his new toy. He'd also farted uncontrollably and when Trace opened the car door, he was nearly knocked off his feet. He started to scold the dog but laughter overwhelmed him. He rolled down all of the windows but when he pulled up to pay the parking fee, the guy at the booth made a face and he was sure it was because he thought Trace was stinking up the truck. Trace roared with laughter as he headed to the emergency room entrance.

Damn dog!

The smell was gone by the time he pulled up, or so he thought. Kiki and the nurse were waiting and he jumped out, running around the truck and picking Kiki up from the chair. He deposited her carefully into the front seat, helping her on with her seatbelt. Climbing back into the truck, he carefully pulled out.

He thought she was asleep, her head resting against the back of the seat and her eyes closed. But she frowned, wrinkled her nose, and groaned.

"Stanley," she scolded. "Quit farting."

Trace couldn't help the giggles. "That dog smells like he's rotting from the inside out."

Kiki grinned, opening her eyes and looking at him. "Sorry," she said. "I should have warned you. I have to give him gas pills daily or this is what happens."

He grinned in return, reaching out to take her hand. He brought it to his lips for a sweet kiss. "Are you awake enough that we can have a conversation?"

She nodded but her eyes were heavy lidded. "They gave me something to knock me out, I think."

"They sure did."

"Are we going back to the house?"

He shook his head. "It's still a crime scene and I don't want you over there right now," he said. "I'm taking you to the Hilton so you can get some sleep. I'm going to back over to the house and repair the broken window."

She lay there, her head against the seat, looking at him. "Why?"

He glanced at her. "Why what?"

"Why are you doing all of this?"

"Because I'm your boyfriend."

"You *are?*"

"Yes."

"I didn't realize I'd given you an answer yet."

"You did. You just don't remember."

She just stared at him. Then, she grinned. "You're a pretty take-charge kind of guy, aren't you?"

He shrugged, perhaps with some regret. "Always. Got a problem with that?"

"No," she said softly. "I'm really touched that you would take the trouble to take care of the dog, of me, and of the house. That's really sweet."

He just lifted her hand and kissed it as they came to a stoplight. Then, he leaned over and pulled her against him, planting a warm and sensual kiss against her mouth. Kiki forgot about her aches, pains, and exhaustion in a split second, her hands finding their way into his soft, cropped hair. The kiss quickly turned heated and sexy, tongues licking and tasting, as the light turned green and someone behind him honked. Trace let her go and drove through the intersection.

"Wow," he exhaled softly, wiping at his mouth. "I could do that again, sometime."

Kiki giggled softly, reaching out to take his hand this time. He squeezed her fingers tightly.

"Me, too," she whispered.

He glanced at her, grinning, before refocusing on the road. "Hey, I've been thinking a few things," he ventured. "Shouldn't you call your mom and dad to let them know what happened?"

Her smile vanished. "Not today," she said. "They'll both freak out and I can't deal with that right now. I'll call them tonight when things have calmed down. I love my parents to death, but they're both worrywarts. I'll never hear the end of it."

"End of what?"

"Moving into that neighborhood," she said. "My dad wasn't so sure about it but my mom was positively averse. If they catch wind of what happened, they're going to put all kinds of pressure on me to sell and get out, and I just don't want to do it."

Trace was silent for a moment, watching the Pasadena Hilton coming up on the left, a block-shaped structure that was taller than almost any building in the city. "They worry about you because you're alone," he said quietly. "You're not alone anymore."

She looked at him. "What do you mean?"

He didn't look at her as he slowed down to make the left-hand turn to pull into the Hilton's front entrance. "I mean that you have me now," he said. "I'm not going to let you live there alone."

Her head came up off the seat. "We've known each other three days and already you're moving in with me?"

He nodded. "As a tenant," he said as he pulled the truck to a stop and looked at her. "Look, I'm not *that* much of an idiot, Katharine. I wouldn't move in with a woman I just met, no matter how wonderful and luscious and sweet she is. You've got a lot of rooms in that big house. I'll sleep in one of those and that way, you won't be alone. You'll have me around. It'll be like a boarding house, only it'll be your boyfriend who's your boarder."

She was serious, torn. "I told you I wouldn't date you if you were working on my house."

"You said you wouldn't date me if you awarded Rocklin the job. You haven't awarded Rocklin anything."

She gave him an expression suggesting it was all semantics. "I don't know..."

"Look—if you don't want to go out with me, just say so."

"Of course I do."

"Then there's nothing more to talk about," he replied with finality. Then, he leaned forward and kissed her tenderly. "Just ask yourself how right this feels. If, at any time, things start getting weird, then we'll address the issues like adults. But meanwhile, just enjoy what's happening, okay? I know I will."

She accepted his kiss, which grew increasingly heated, until she realized the bellboys were coming out to greet the truck. She pulled back from him, her lips red from his attention, her eyes riveted to the young men in Hilton uniforms.

"I don't have any luggage," she said. "In fact, I don't have anything but the pajamas I'm wearing. I don't even have shoes."

He caught a glimpse of the bellboys as well. "So what? We'll fix that."

"But what about Stanley? We can't just leave him here."

"I'll sneak him in after we check in."

Before she could reply, he climbed out of the truck, went around to the other side, and opened her door. Kiki gingerly tried to climb out, putting her feet on the wet pavement, but he scooped her up in his arms before she could get out and carried her on into the lobby.

The front desk clerk looked at them both a little strangely when they checked in but said nothing. She handed over the room keys but Trace diverted into the gift shop as they headed to the elevators. Fifteen minutes later, Kiki emerged with an adorable pair of casual pants and a matching top, an equally adorable pair of animal print shoes, a loungewear outfit that was comfy and trendy, earrings, make-up, and all of the toiletries she could handle. Trace even bought her a robe. It was an expensive purchase but he didn't bat an eyelash. He just got her what she wanted and carried the booty up to her room on the ninth floor.

It would have been very easy to stay with her in the room but he thought better of it. He didn't want to wreck their budding relationship with too-soon sex or related foreplay. In fact, he really wanted to take his time with her and get to know her before taking that huge step. But he had to admit, it would be difficult to pace himself. He was already so attracted to her that he could barely control it. Once he got her into bed, he knew he'd be lost forever.

Moreover, Kiki was truly exhausted and still in the throes of the sedative. Trace put her in bed himself, covered her up, and pulled the curtains closed so it was completely dark in the room. As she dozed, he went back down to the truck, moved it around the corner, and then brought Stanley and his goodies in through a side entrance. He managed to get the dog up to the room without anyone seeing him, putting him in bed next to Kiki. She was genuinely touched at Trace's efforts as she snuggled with her dog.

However, she seemed to get anxious again at the thought of him leaving her alone, so he sat on the bed next to her, stroking her beautiful hair, until she finally fell into an exhausted sleep. Only then did he tiptoe out of the room, leaving his business card on the nightstand with his cell phone number circled and a note promising he'd be back by noon.

He was a man on a mission.

NINE

"DAD'S LOOKING FOR YOU," Jesse said. "Where in the hell are you?"

Trace was standing on Kiki's back porch with two glass guys, watching the installation of the new back window. He had answered his brother's call and now was faced with the question he had been waiting for all morning. *Where in the hell are you?* A workaholic with basically no personal life, he was always the first one in the office and the last one to leave; therefore, his absence would be noted.

Cell phone to his ear, he turned away from the glass workers and walked into the old kitchen. It seemed so empty without Kiki and that farting dog.

"Jess, I don't even know where to start," he muttered to his brother. "It's all happened so fast I haven't had a chance to talk to you about it."

"Talk to me about what?" Jesse wanted to know. "Look, we had a meeting with the people from Cal Tech a half hour ago. You were supposed to be in on that meeting, remember?"

Trace nodded. "I remember," he said. "But this couldn't be helped."

"*What* couldn't be helped?" Jesse was getting irritated. "Start making sense."

Trace found one of the two stools in the kitchen and lowered himself onto it. "Okay, here goes," he said. "But don't tell Dad, okay? This is something I need to tell him myself."

"Uh...okay. What's going on?"

Trace collected his thoughts before continuing. "You remember that I did an estimate on Jim Wickham's sister's house?"

"Yes, the one that Dad originally did."

"Right," Trace continued. "I don't even know how to say this, but somewhere over the past three days, we've fallen for each other."

Jesse didn't catch on right away. "What do you mean you've...oh. Wait—*what?* What do you mean?"

Trace sighed. "Just what I said," he replied. "She's a wonderful woman and I'm crazy about her, like I've never been crazy about anyone in my life."

On the other end of the phone, Jesse's mouth was hanging open. "Are you *insane?*" he asked. "Is this the same brother who swore off women forever?"

"The same."

"The one who said he'd never get close to anyone ever again?"

"Yes."

"But you've only known the woman for three days!"

"It doesn't matter. It's been the best three days of my life. Look, I can't explain it to you any better than that. I met a woman and…Jess, it was like love at first sight. I've never known anything like that in my entire life."

Jesse was having a difficult time processing what he was hearing. He finally gave up, at least for the moment. "Really?" he said, his tone going from outraged to incredulous. "I don't even know what to say to that. I would have never expected to hear that from you in a million years."

Trace couldn't disagree. "I know," he muttered. "So you wanted to know where I am. I'll tell you—this morning, I was heading over to her house before heading in to work and as I pulled up, there were cop cars and ambulances all over the damn place. Turns out someone broke into her house last night and she ended up killing the guy in self-defense, so I've been with her at the hospital all morning. Right now, I'm with the glass contractor having a new window put in to replace the one that was smashed in the break-in."

He could hear Jesse hiss. "Oh, my God," he said. "That's terrible. Is she okay?"

"Yes," Trace replied. "She's okay, but she's understandably shaken up and I want to secure the house for her to make her feel safer. I…I just really need to do this, you know? I want to help her."

"I get it," Jesse replied, his manner considerably softer than it had been moments earlier. "Wow, dude…it sounds like you really got yourself tangled up in the start of something."

Trace grinned. "It's *all* good, trust me," he said. "I'll call Dad in a while, but until then, don't say anything to him, okay?"

"I won't," Jesse said. "Do you need any help? Want me to come over there and give you a hand?"

Trace looked around the kitchen, at the utility porch where the guys were sealing up the glass, and started thinking. "If you can spare an hour," he said. "Come on over. Maybe you can help me figure out how to make this place more secure."

"What's the address?"

"899 North Raymond Avenue in Pasadena."

"I'm on my way."

"Thanks, Jess."

He heard his brother snort on the other end. "You big dummy," he said. "I just don't want to see you get in over your head."

Trace chuckled and hung up the phone. He felt better with his younger, and very astute, brother coming over to figure out what more security measures they could do quickly on the house. He knew Kiki was going to want to return immediately. This was her house and she was going to live in it.

With a sigh, he headed to the second floor where the cleaning crew was just finishing up in the master bedroom. It was a specialty cleaning service Detective Irwin had recommended, one used to clean up crime scenes. The blood and gore was gone, the floors and walls sanitized, and they were bleaching out the old grout on the floor as a final step to remove any residual brown stains. Fortunately, it hadn't been a horrible mess, but bad enough. As Trace stood in the doorway and watched them finish up, he had to admit it looked great.

He could hear voices downstairs. Assuming it was the glass guys getting ready to leave, he headed downstairs and realized the voices were coming from the front of the house. Peering out of the front door, he saw two young women standing near the old fountain. They were looking around, wandering up to the front door. He opened the front door wide.

"Hi," he said simply.

The girls came to a halt. They looked confused, then they looked at each other, and started giggling.

"Hi," one replied. She was giggling uncontrollably. "Sorry. I thought...isn't this 899 North Raymond?"

Trace nodded. "Yes," he replied. "Are you looking for someone?"

The girls were very giggly. "Yes," the girl replied. "My mom. I'm looking for Kiki Conrad."

Trace grinned when he realized who the girls were, but in the same breath, he was very surprised to see them. Kiki had made no mention that her girls were coming home and he was pretty sure she wouldn't want them walking into the tail end of a crime scene.

"This is her home," he said. "I'm Trace Rocklin. I'm her...contractor."

The girls were still giggling as they approached, the more talkative of the pair extending her hand.

"Embry Conrad," she said. "This is my sister, Esme."

Trace shook their hands, one after the other. Although they looked similar, they weren't identical - Embry looked a good deal like her mother with honey-colored hair and brown eyes, while Esme was slightly taller and had bright blue eyes and brown hair. They were gorgeous young women, no doubt. He began to wonder what he was going to tell them about their mother's whereabouts and set forth on that subject right away so the girls wouldn't suspect anything odd. Whatever they were told about the situation, Trace was determined, would have to come from Kiki.

"Your mom..." He stopped and cleared his throat. "She's at a hotel in town. The house had some damage and I've been working to make it livable for her."

"Really?" Esme stepped up on the porch, very interested in the structure. "What kind of damage? It looks really old."

"It is." Trace followed her as she headed into the house. "Did your mom know you were coming? She didn't mention anything."

The girls both shook their head, in unison. "Classes are cancelled today so we drove up from San Diego this morning," Esme said. "We wanted to see Mom's new house. We wanted to surprise her."

Surprise! Trace thought ironically. He stood in the open doorway as the girls wandered through the big sitting room and the connecting rooms beyond. The glass contractors were still making some noise so Trace's story about fixing a "damaged" house held some truth. But he was worried about the cleaners upstairs and was preparing himself for their questions when the cleaners suddenly began coming down the stairs with all of their equipment.

"All finished," the supervisor said as he lugged his wet-dry vacuum down the stairs. "We were able to get all of the stains out and then use a biohazard solvent to clean up any traces of body fluids. Take a look at it and make sure you're happy with the job before we leave."

Trace didn't dare look at the girls. He took the steps, two at a time, and walked quickly into the master bedroom, examined it with all due haste, before making his way downstairs again.

"It looks fine," he told them. "I gave you my card, right?"

The supervisor nodded. "I have it."

"Send me an invoice at that address."

The cleaning crew thanked him and hauled all of their stuff out of the house. By the time he turned around to look at the girls, they were gazing at him with some suspicion. *Here it comes*, he thought.

"What happened?" Embry asked.

Trace sighed uneasily. He didn't want to lie to them, but he didn't want to overstep his bounds, either. He gave them a rather indecisive expression.

"Do you want to see your mom?" he asked, avoiding the question.

Both girls nodded. "Where is she?" Embry asked.

Trace held out a hand to beg them for a moment's pause while he went back to the glass contractor and told the man to lock the house up when he was finished. Then he dug his keys out of his pocket and headed out to the front of the house.

"Where did you park?" he asked.

Embry pointed out to the curb in front of the house. "Out there."

Trace motioned to them. "Follow me, then," he headed out the front door. "I'll take you to your mom."

The girls trotted after him, but it was clear they were confused and apprehensive. "Wait a minute," Esme said, even though she was following him. "Is my mom okay?"

"Your mom is fine," Trace said calmly. "I told you she was staying in a hotel a few miles away because I needed to repair some damage to the house."

"But what did that guy say about body fluid?" Embry rushed up beside him as they made their way out into the front yard. "What did he mean?"

Trace shrugged, not looking at her as they neared the old wrought iron gate that led to the sidewalk. "I'm just the contractor," he said. "You'd better ask your mom those questions."

The girls were still apprehensive and confused. "Hold on," Embry said flatly. "We don't even know you. We're not going anywhere with you."

He came to a halt, turning to look at them. "You're going to follow me in your car to the Pasadena Hilton," he told them. "Your mother's room is nine-thirty-one. I will give you the key and you can go into the hotel yourself and up to her room. I won't follow you, walk with you, or anything else, I promise. I'll just take you to her. Okay?"

The girls looked at him dubiously, then at each other. Finally, Embry shrugged. "Okay," she said. "But no funny stuff, okay? Anything weird and I'll start screaming like a bitch. I'll attract more attention than you can handle. Get it?"

Trace fought off a grin. "Got it."

Embry's gaze lingered on him. "Good," she agreed, but it was stern. "Then let's go."

Trace did as he was told.

The girls had awoken their mother, and the dog, when they let themselves into the hotel room. Given what had just happened to Kiki, and the fact that she was startled out of a deep sleep, they also scared the crap out of their mother, sending her into hysteria until she realized who it was. After that, there were a lot of tears from their mom as the reasons for her being in a hotel room came tumbling out. The girls were traumatized right along with their mother.

But Trace hadn't known any of that. He had taken the girls to the hotel, given them a key, and then waited a nominal amount of time out in the driveway in case they needed him before heading back to the house. Since the girls had a car, a cute yellow Volkswagen Beetle that suited them perfectly, he knew Kiki had transportation should she need it.

It felt odd for him to head back to the house and not go up and check on Kiki, but he didn't want to push himself on her any more than he was already doing. He'd been rather bossy about their entire relationship up until this point, but now with her girls around, he thought it best to back off and let Kiki take the lead as far as her children were concerned. Everything was still so new, so exciting, and so uncertain.

So he went back to the house where the glass contractor had just finished sealing off the glass. Trace told the guy to send him an invoice, checking the glass for workmanship as the glass people packed up and left. Alone in Kiki's house, he decided the next order of business was to figure out how to make the property more secure. The current state didn't prevent a drug addict from breaking in and trying to kill Kiki, so he wandered outside and began to roam.

He wanted to make it fool-proof.

To begin with, the property was fairly sizable. It was also surrounded by a massive, unkempt hedge that ran the entire perimeter of the property except for the garage area. That, and the driveway, was open to the street, which he didn't like in the least. In this neighborhood, it was like an open invitation for trouble. As he was standing back by the garage, he caught sight of movement near the house.

Jesse was walking around the side of the structure, looking over the house, the yard, and anything else. His attention was everywhere. Trace let out a sharp, brief whistle between his teeth and Jesse finally caught sight of him. The tall, partially-balding brother waved as he made his way over.

"Man," he hissed. "This is a hell of a place. Looks like Herman and Lily Munster live here."

Trace gave him a half-grin. "No joke," he agreed. "The glass contractor just finished up and I was standing out here trying to figure out what we could do, inexpensively, to secure the property so another crackhead can't crash the place. Come on and walk with me."

Jesse did. He noted the old, wrought iron fence and the massive growth of hedge that grew around it. He and his brother strolled across the grass and hacked through the jungle of overgrowth that Kiki had been trying to clear out on the south side of the front yard. They traipsed through the ivy that covered most of the west side of the front yard and out onto the sidewalk before they began to get a grasp of how the perimeter fence was laid out. Jesse began to point.

"This place isn't all that insecure," he said. "Look at this fence; it's sturdy wrought iron and about nine feet high. See the spikes on the ends? The hedge covers that detail up. You can't scale it."

Trace was nodding as his brother spoke. He put his hands on his hips and looked around the yard. "You know what I think?" he said. "I think that guy just came in off the driveway. It's wide open to the street and the gate lock is busted. He just walked right in because, seriously, I can't see any other way for someone to get on this property. This fence is impossible to scale."

Jesse nodded as they began heading back to the garage area. "We can go get a chain lock right now from the hardware store and secure the back gate," he said. "We could also get about ten twenty-gallon juniper trees and plant them along the garage fence to give the house some privacy from that open driveway. Once those things grow in, you won't be able to see a thing.

Trace agreed. "That will take care of securing this yard, at least for now," he said. "We need to get a lock on that front gate, too."

Jesse eyed the gate. "I would suggest getting an entirely new gate, period. That one isn't all that steady."

Trace nodded, thinking of a few fence contractors he was going to call. Then he began moving toward the house. "Come inside and see this beast. It's really something."

Jesse followed him inside. He was met by the smell of must, dust, and over a century of old wood and plaster. From the floor to the built-in hutch in the dining room, built-in bench in the entry way, and every single wall of the house, it was old beyond old. Jesse's eyebrows flew up.

"Holy smokes," he exclaimed softly. "Look at this place."

Trace was by the stairs, running his hand on the intricately carved banister. "I know," he said. "Take a look at this staircase and the medallion on the ceiling with the light fixture hanging out of it. They don't make them like that anymore."

Jesse couldn't keep his mouth from hanging open.

"Amazing," he said, noticing the windows. "Look at the Tiffany windows. Original?"

"Probably."

Jesse looked around again and began wandering. "This built-in hutch is incredible," he said, running his hands over the wood. "Look at the key holes for the drawers; every one of them is etched bronze."

Trace grinned at his brother, so entranced by the old house. "Look at the doorknobs," he said, pointing to the old door that led into the kitchen. "Crystal doorknobs and etched bronze fixtures. I could go on and on. Original flooring in the kitchen and throughout the house, stained glass windows in the dining room, and then upstairs there are four big bathrooms with all original tile and clawfoot tubs. The guy that built this place spared no expense, that's for sure. In its day, it must have been a hell of a showplace."

Jesse wriggled his eyebrows. "That's an understatement," he said. "Show me the house."

Trace did, as if the thing belonged to him and he was eager to show it off. In fact, he felt a certain pride showing the place, even in its run-down state, because, even in its present condition, it didn't matter. It was still a jewel of a house, waiting to shine again.

Trace took his brother all around the downstairs, showed him the walls, the hutches, the original light fixtures, and then took him upstairs to see the five large bedrooms. He even took him up in the attic. All in all, Jesse was more in love with the place than Kiki probably was and he has a host of ideas on how to fix the place up. But Trace had to call him off, reminding him that they were only there to ensure the perimeter was secured.

Locking the house up, they jumped into Trace's truck and headed down to the home supply store that was about a half-mile away. They picked up chains and padlocks, wandering out into the garden section and seeing that the store happened to have several giant shrubberies, all over six feet high. When Jesse tracked down an employee, the man said they had just gotten the shipment in, so Jesse and Trace bought ten of them to cover the back fence and provide some privacy off the driveway. Trace couldn't get them all in his truck so they had to make two runs to bring everything back. And with that, the brothers dug in for the afternoon.

They had their work cut out for them.

TEN

KIKI WANTED TO GO HOME.

After spending the afternoon with her daughters holed up in the Hilton, she made the decision to go home. Nothing was going to drive her out of her new home, including a violent crime. She could have very easily stayed away for weeks, going to her parents' house and cowering from the monstrosity she had purchased and the bad event that had happened within the old walls, but she just couldn't do it. Kiki was a fighter by nature and she and that old house, and that shady neighborhood, were going to come to terms.

Her terms.

She called Trace's number twice but it went to voicemail. Curious as to where he was, not to mention disappointed that he hadn't answered his phone, she took a shower, washed her hair and cleaned up, and put on the cute clothing he'd bought her. Meanwhile, Esme and

Embry had ordered room service so by the time she emerged from the bathroom the girls had quite a spread set out. Smelling the food reminded Kiki that she hadn't eaten all day so while the girls tucked into sandwiches and fries, she confiscated the cheeseburger and wolfed it down.

Fed, bathed, and satisfied, she packed up her meager items into the big paper bag from the gift shop and followed the girls outside to their Volkswagen. Esme carried Stanley out with some stealth, as dogs weren't allowed in the hotel, while Embry opened up the car. It had stopped raining and, at sunset, the sky was clear and bright. Kiki, her girls, and the dog climbed into the car and sped off for northwest Pasadena.

When they pulled up to the curb outside the front of the house, they couldn't see any activity. It was a big, foreboding house that was shadowed and rather creepy as the sun set. As Kiki climbed out of the car with the dog, the girls grabbed their suitcases and bags from the trunk.

"Mom?" Embry was looking up at the old house as her mother opened the big front gate. "I'm kind of scared to come back here after what happened to you this morning. Are you sure it's safe?"

They wandered down the path that led to the fountain and, beyond that, the porch. Kiki was trying not to let on that her sense of fear was returning. The last time she was in this house, a man had tried to kill her.

"It'll be fine," she assured them. "Mr. Rocklin said he would secure the house and I believe him. What happened was just a freak thing, girls. I don't want you getting worked up about it."

"Mr. Rocklin," Esme giggled. "So...what did you do, Mom? Run an ad for the hottest contractor to come fix your house?"

Kiki bit her lip, grinning, as she put Stanley down so he could relieve himself. "I did, actually," she teased back. She hadn't told the girls anything about Trace yet because their focus had been on what had happened and not much else. Now, the questions were coming and she tried to be prepared. "Actually, he and Uncle Jimmy were best friends back in high school. Gramma and Grampa know the family."

"Really?" Esme said, interested. "He's really cute."

Kiki pulled out her house key, watching Embry chase after the dog. "He's a very nice man."

"How long is he going to be working on the house?" Esme asked.

Kiki shrugged. "To tell you the truth, I haven't even awarded his company the job yet. It's pretty pricey. I'm not sure what I'm going to do."

"Then what's he doing here?"

"I told you—he's a friend of Uncle Jimmy's and he's helping me out."

Embry picked up the dog and picked her way over through the bramble. "Is he married?"

Esme giggled and Kiki grinned. "I think he's a little old for you," she said.

Embry laughed. "No, Mom," she insisted, "for *you*."

Kiki just grinned and shook her head. She didn't want to respond to her daughter, mostly because she wasn't sure what to say. But she knew she was going to have to figure out something fast considering Trace had pretty much moved himself into the house. Just as they reached the front door, they began hearing commotion in the back yard. Their smiles faded.

"What's that?" Esme wanted to know, looking at her mother.

Kiki could hear the voices, the banging about. She shook her head. "I don't know," she said as she handed the house key to Esme. "Open up the house. I'll be right back."

The girls did as they were told as Kiki walked around the side of the house. Cautiously, she made her way across the overgrown brick, straining to catch a glimpse of what was causing the noise until the back yard came into view. She could immediately see two big pickup trucks in her driveway and a host of equipment. Additionally, someone was planting some fairly heavy shrubbery all along her back fence. Curious, she made her way over to the fence only to be confronted with a man she'd never seen before.

Jesse was covered with dirt, wearing massive gloves with a post hole digger in his hand. He had been digging away at a hole for one of the shrubs, coming up for air and coming face to face with a decidedly beautiful woman. Startled, he accidentally dropped the post hole digger.

"Uh...hi," he said, reaching down to quickly pick up the equipment. "I'm Jesse Rocklin, Rocklin Construction."

About the time he said it, Trace heard him but he

couldn't see who he was talking to because of all the bushes. Stripped from the waist up, he was sweaty and dirty and tanned and gorgeous. At least, that's what Kiki thought when he came around a large bush and they caught sight of each other. The man looked like one of those guys on the "Sexy Construction Workers" calendar.

Holy smokes!

"Hi," Trace said with surprise. "What are you doing back?"

Kiki wasn't quite over the sight of him in all of his half-naked glory. "I didn't want to stay at the hotel any longer," she said, distracted by all that flesh. "Besides, the girls wanted to see the house and I really wanted to come home. What are you guys doing?"

Trace propped his shovel up against the fence and pulled off his gloves as he made his way over to her.

"How are you feeling?" he asked, his tone soft.

It was difficult to look him in the eye when his beautiful, muscular chest was right in her face. She gazed up at him.

"Better," she said softly. "Thank you for being so wonderful and taking care of everything."

He smiled at her, the warmth between them sparking wildly. "Anything for you," he murmured, his gaze drifting over her lovely face. "You're sure you're okay?"

"Fine."

"Where are your daughters?"

"In the house." She wriggled her eyebrows. "They've been asking about you. I think you made an impression."

He chuckled nervously, scratching his head. "I'm not sure how," he said. "We didn't say a whole lot to each other. I just tried to keep them from finding out what went on this morning. I figured it was your place to tell them."

Her smile faded. "I told them," she said. "I had to. When they let themselves into the hotel room, they startled me so badly that I freaked out. I had to tell them why their mom was plastered to the ceiling, screaming her head off."

He nodded, his gaze drifting up to the big, imposing house. "The window's repaired, at any rate," he said, then turned to his brother, who had resumed digging holes. "My brother and I have been working on securing the yard. Jesse, this is Kiki Conrad in case you haven't figured that out yet."

Jesse stopped digging and grinned. "Actually, I did."

Kiki smiled in return. "It's very nice to meet you."

Jesse leaned on his digger. "You, too," he said. "So you're Jimmy's little sister?"

"And you're Trace's little brother?"

Jesse laughed. "Touché, my friend," he said, already feeling comfortable with her. His gaze moved to the house. "I really love your house. I want to marry it."

Kiki giggled. "You'll have to get in line," she told him. "I'm in love with it so I get first dibs."

Jesse made a face. "I thought you were in love with my brother?"

Kiki's laughter grew and her cheeks went warm. She

put a hand to her face, looking at Trace. "Did you tell him that?"

Trace was smiling, shaking his head. "I did *not*," he said, looking at his brother. "He's pretty close to being duct-taped to a chair and getting a beating if he doesn't shut his mouth."

Jesse grinned as he resumed digging with his post hole digger. "Eh, you don't scare me, you big bully," he sneered, although it was in good humor. "You're not going to do anything with her around."

Kiki snorted as Trace just shook his head. "Sorry," he said. "He's kind of a pain. Nobody in the family likes him."

"I can tell," Kiki said, though she didn't mean a word of it. She could see how easy the brothers were with each other. She motioned to the shrubbery. "So, what are you doing here?"

Trace shifted to the subject of the project. "Providing you some protection and privacy," he said. "Jesse and I figured that the guy who broke in must have come in off the driveway because there's really no barrier of protection here. It's the weak link in the security. Therefore, we bought a lock for the back gate and are planting these shrubs to provide a measure of privacy from the street. We're going to make this place as private and as bottled-up as we can get it."

By this time, Kiki's smile was gone. "You would do all of this?"

He turned to look at her, feeling his heart soften as he gazed into her sweet face. "Of course I would," he said, his voice softening. "I want to make sure you feel safe and secure here. This is only the beginning."

Kiki wasn't quite sure what to say. She looked at the shrubs and, as touched as she was, all she could see was dollar signs. She was already worried what she owed him.

"My gosh," she breathed. "I'm not quite sure what to say. That you'd go to so much trouble..."

He cut her off, gently done. "It wasn't any trouble at all," he assured her. "We'll be done in a half hour or so. Can I take you and the girls to dinner when I'm done?"

She looked at him. Really looked at him. It was a pivotal moment - if she truly wanted to date him as she said she did, then she would have to tell her girls something about her relationship with him, infantile as it was. But if she was unsure, then this moment would tell the tale. Given his actions over the past twelve hours, she had come to see that he was as genuine as they come. His actions had spoken far louder than words. If she had any reservation about their relationship, however small, it was gone.

"I should probably tell them something...about us," she said. "Are you still planning on moving in?"

"I'm going to go home after dinner and pull some things together."

"Are you sure?"

"You're not spending another night alone in this house. I'll sleep on the damn porch if I have to, but you're not going to be alone."

She sighed faintly, a smile on her lips. "All right," she

agreed. "Give me a few minutes to let the girls know...well, let them know what's going on. It's only fair."

His eyes glimmered. "I'll follow your lead with them."

It was a scary and thrilling prospect, like they were taking the next big step. She nodded and he winked at her. As she turned for the gate and he turned back for his shovel, Kiki called over to Jesse.

"It was good to meet you, little brother," she said, watching him as he looked up from his shovel and grinned. "You're welcome to come back any time."

"I'll take you up on that," he said as he waved at her.

Kiki went back into the yard, listening to the digging and scraping going on behind her. By the time she reached the back door, she noticed the brand-new window. She also noticed two faces gazing back at her from inside. Esme opened the back door for her mother.

"What are they doing out there?" she asked as Kiki came into the house. "Is that Mr. Rocklin? Oh, my God... does he have his *shirt* off?"

Kiki shut the back door to prevent Trace from hearing Esme's teenage lust, then glanced out of the big, new window. "It's Mr. Rocklin and his brother," she said, not addressing the missing shirt question. Then she turned around to face the girls. "Do you want to see the house now?"

The distraction worked because they very much wanted to see the house. Kiki gave them the grand tour of the ground floor before taking them upstairs to the old bedrooms and bathrooms. She got the willies when she passed into her bedroom, remembering the state she last saw it in, but it was cleaned and sanitized, and it was easy to forget that she last saw it with a body in it. In fact, showing the girls the house brought around her love of the old place again and she pushed the horror out of her mind. She wasn't going to let it lick her.

Kiki took the girls up to the attic and explained that she was going to make it their "space." They loved the idea and began planning out where they were going to put their beds and desks. Kiki stood over by the attic window that looked over the back yard, watching her daughters as they paced around the attic. She was also watching Trace and Jesse, still digging out by the driveway. They had planted enough six-foot shrubs to very adequately block the view of the back yard from the driveway. She was mostly watching Trace in all of his naked-torso glory. It had easily been over five years since she last had sex and she couldn't help but think about what it would be like to be intimate with him.

She sincerely hoped she got to find out.

"Mom?" Esme said. "Did you hear me?"

Kiki tore her gaze from the window, noticing that both of her children were looking curiously at her. She smiled weakly.

"I didn't," she said. "What did you say?"

The girls gravitated over toward the window to see what had their mother's attention. It didn't take either of them long to figure out that she was watching Trace. There was nothing else she could possibly be looking at that intently. The girls eyed the shirtless man with the fabulous torso.

"I asked if we could paint it pink on one wall and do a zebra print on the other," Esme said, grinning knowingly at her sister.

Kiki opened her mouth to flatly refuse them but she saw that they were teasing her. She could also see that they were looking out of the window just as she was. Her girls were silly but they weren't dense. She suspected they could already see their mother's attraction to Trace Rocklin. In fact, she was sure they knew it. They were young women now, maturing admirably, and not little children that needed to be protected.

The time for truth had come.

"I'm finding myself in a strange position," she finally said.

Esme, in particular, was eyeing Trace as the man used his muscles to plant the last juniper. "Why?" she asked.

Kiki reached out and stroked Embry's long hair. "Because...I mean, you know what went on with Daddy when he died."

The girls sobered. "We know," Embry, the more mature and outspoken of the pair, murmured softly. "We know what you went through. We also know how much you tried to protect us from it."

Kiki was serious. "I just didn't want your memories of your dad to be damaged."

"We know," Embry said. "They weren't. He is still our dad and we will always love him."

Kiki thought about Mark Conrad for a moment. "He was a pretty good guy," she said. "I still miss him sometimes."

"Even after you found out...you know, what went on?" Embry wanted to know.

Kiki nodded. "He was still a good husband and provider," she said. "I miss his smile. Do you remember it? So bright. He had the best smile."

The girls grinned; Embry had his smile. "Dad looked like an ad for toothpaste," she said. "Remember how he used to leave dental floss all over the house?"

Kiki rolled her eyes in recollection, her attention returning to the window and Trace as he and his brother began to pack up their equipment. She sobered.

"I will admit, though, that Daddy and I didn't have the greatest relationship the last few years he was alive," she said softly. "He was distant from me, always busy. I felt like a single parent a lot of the time. Lonely, you know? I pretty much resigned myself to the fact that it was going to be that way the rest of my life, but it looks like I might have been wrong."

"Why?" Esme wanted to know.

Kiki pointed out the window, to Trace and Jesse as they loaded up one of the pickup trucks in the driveway.

"I was acquainted with Trace Rocklin back in high school," she said. "As I told you, he and Uncle Jimmy were best friends. I remember Trace as this big, quiet kid that used to hang around Gramma and Grampa's house but not much more than that until he showed up here a few days ago to give me an estimate to restore the house. Right away, it was like we 'clicked'. He's handsome and funny and very thoughtful. When all of that chaos happened this morning, he was so strong. He took care of me and took care of Stanley. He really seems to be a man of his word and I respect that. I like him a lot."

The girls were torn between surprise and glee. "Does he like you?" Esme asked.

"He wants to be my boyfriend."

"I *knew* it," Embry said as her suspicions had just been confirmed. "This morning when we came looking for you, there was something in his face when he talked about you. So...are you going to go out with him?"

"Would you have a problem if I did?"

Esme started giggling but Embry shook her head. "You *should* go out with him," she insisted. "I know you've been lonely since Dad died and all. Besides, Mr. Rocklin is really hot!"

Esme's giggles turned to laughter. Embry started laughing, too. Kiki grinned at her girls, realizing that, somehow, they'd grown up since the last time she saw them. She could hear it in their voices and see it in their manner. They were accepting of the situation, of their mother's needs, something that only came with maturity. She was glad to see it and also relieved.

"I don't know where it's going," she said honestly. "Maybe it goes nowhere. Maybe we end up...well, you know...together forever or married. But for now, I'm going to enjoy it and I wanted to be up front with you girls about what's going on. Are you sure you're okay with it?"

The girls nodded seriously. "We're fine with it," Embry said.

"Good," Kiki said, "because there's more. Because of what happened this morning, Trace wants to move in here with me. But it's not what you think—he's going to rent a room and help me work on the place. He really just doesn't want me being alone."

The girls looked at each other. Embry finally wriggled her eyebrows. "Mom, what would you say if I moved in with a guy I'd only known three days?"

"I'd yell at you and then send you to live in a convent."

Embry shrugged. "I'm not going to yell at you, but maybe you should re-think living with a guy you just met. I mean, he's really cute and all, but that's a big step."

Kiki shook her head. "It's not like that," she assured them. "Think of this house as an apartment building. He's going to live in one apartment and I'm going to live in another. It's not going to be like we're shacking up. We're not even going to share the same bedroom. Besides, after what happened this morning...I admit I'm not looking forward to spending another night alone."

"So he's an emotional crutch?" Embry pressed.

Kiki shook her head. "Not at all," she replied. "He's a man I'd like to get to know very well."

"I still say you should get to know him better first."

Kiki gazed at her daughter, mulling over the suggestion. Then she reached out and pulled the young lady to her, kissing her head.

"When in the hell did you grow up?" she muttered as she kissed her again.

Before Embry could reply, Esme caught sight of Trace and Jesse as they headed back into the yard. "Mom," she said. "They're done. He's coming to the house."

"Let's go see Mr. Sexy!" Embry exclaimed.

Kiki let go of Embry so fast that the young girl stumbled. Then, they were a giggling herd of women as they raced down from the attic, to the second floor, and down to the first floor. Stanley, who had been sleeping on his bed in the kitchen, heard the thundering feet and started to bark. About the time they reached the kitchen, there was a knock on the back door and Embry gently pushed her mother out of the way, playfully, and ran to the back door with her sister on her heels. Giggling and breathless, they opened the door.

Trace, with his shirt on now, stood there with Jesse, wondering why the girls were so giddy. He grinned.

"Whatever's going on in there, it sounds like a good time," he observed.

The girls started laughing as Kiki came up behind them and pushed between the pair. "They're out of control," she told him, not wanting to explain why her girls were so giggly. "Are you finished?"

She was shifting the subject and Trace went with her. "Yes," he replied. "Do you want to come out and take a look to see if we missed anything?"

Kiki shrugged as she stepped outside. "I really wouldn't know," she said. "You guys did this on your own, so if you like it, I like it. What do I owe you?"

"A couple of bottles of water," Jesse said. "We did it as one old family friend to another."

Kiki shook her head firmly. "No way, you guys," she said, even as Embry ran for the refrigerator to get them water. "That had to cost you at least a couple of hundred dollars. Please let me pay you for it."

Embry stuck her long arms in between her mother and Trace, handing him and Jesse the water. Trace accepted it gratefully.

"How 'bout you pay for dinner?" he said, his eyes glimmering at her. "We'll call it even."

"Done."

"Jesse's coming, too."

"He'd better."

The men downed the water, handing her back the bottles. "I need to go home and shower," Trace told her. "Where do you want to go eat?"

Kiki cocked her head thoughtfully. "There's that log cabin restaurant out in east Pasadena near the freeway," she said. "The one with the big boat in front of it?"

Trace nodded. "I haven't been there in years, but I love it," he said. "Jesse and I'll meet you there at six?"

"We'll be there."

"Good."

Trace wanted to kiss her goodbye. He really did. It

must have been written all over his face because Embry suddenly shoved her sister back into the kitchen.

"The love birds want to be alone," she said, rather exaggeratedly. "Come on - let's go find something to do."

She made kissing noises as she pushed her giggling sister away. Kiki grinned, embarrassed, as Trace laughed softly. Jesse, sensing he was no longer needed or wanted, turned back for the trucks. Trace watched his brother go before returning his attention to Kiki.

"Am I that obvious?" he asked softly. "I thought I was being kind of cool about it."

"Cool about what?"

"Wanting to kiss you."

Kiki just shrugged. "The girls are just being silly," she replied quietly. "I had a little talk with them."

"I can tell," he grinned. "How did they react?"

"Happy, for the most part," she replied, eyeing him. "But they weren't so sure about you moving in here with me. I explained the arrangement and told them that we wouldn't be sharing a bedroom but that didn't seem to ease them."

He was gazing at her, his hazel eyes glimmering warmly. "They're not stupid."

Her eyes widened. "Now, wait a minute...."

He laughed softly, cutting her off. "I'm just teasing," he said. Then, he grasped her arm gently as he looked at his watch. "If I'm going to meet you there at six, I'd better get going."

He pulled Kiki to him and kissed her on the cheek. Kiki fought off a grin, putting a hand to her cheek as he let her go and headed back to the driveway where the trucks were. Closing the door, she followed her giggly daughters upstairs to get ready for their dinner date.

ELEVEN

TRACE HAD a nice little home in Monrovia, California, up near the mountains. It had been built in 1935 and he had taken the time to restore it when he'd moved in a few years ago. It had beautiful hardwood floors, sleek walls, and a state-of-the-art kitchen because he liked to cook. Cooking reminded him of his grandmother when he was young and all of the comforts of her kitchen. He liked the peace he felt as he broiled fish or made a fancy casserole because it took him back to his childhood. His brothers reaped the benefits because, as a single man, he really had nobody to cook for other than himself and his brothers.

Entering the house through the side door on the drive-way, he tossed his keys on the kitchen counter and continued into the hallway. His master bedroom was big, new, and had a big, marble bathroom. The room, like the house, was sparingly furnished because a bachelor lived there. He only had enough in the house to make it comfortable, but he had sleek, new, flat screen televisions in every room, including the kitchen. Media gadgets were his vice.

As he began pulling off his clothes so he could get into the shower, his cell phone rang. Picking up the phone, he glanced at the incoming number. It was familiar, but one he hadn't seen in a very long time. In fact, he didn't particularly like seeing it at all. After a pause, perhaps one of reluctance, he sighed and answered the call.

"Rocklin," he said.

There was a slight hesitation on the other end. "Trace? It's Harry."

Trace was already unhappy. There was no good reason why Harry King should be calling him. His association with Harry had ended the day he resigned from the CIA two years ago. He had a sinking feeling as he sat heavily on his bed.

"Harry," he greeted steadily. "It's been a long time."

"Long enough," Harry replied. A brilliant man in his fifties, he had a voice like James Earl Jones. "Sorry it couldn't be longer. How are things with you out there in California?"

"Great," Trace replied. "How are things in D.C.?"

"The same," Harry replied. "This shit never changes."

"So why the call? What's going on?"

Trace wasn't going to beat around the bush. The man had called for a reason. On the other end of the line, he could hear Harry sigh.

"Well," he said, "we've been hearing things that may or

may not relate to you. I thought I'd better let you know so you're at least on your guard."

"What things?"

"Nevredev," he replied, somewhat quietly. "That old subject is rearing its head again."

Trace sighed heavily and closed his eyes for a moment. "That's a dead subject to me, Harry," he said. "I'm not going to get back into it."

"You may not have a choice."

Trace's jaw ticked. "It's over," he said. "It was a botched assassination attempt that got Marcos killed. I'm done with all of that and you know it."

Harry's voice was steely. "You are a former covert operations agent, Trace," he said. "You will never be done with this and you know it. All of those men you assassinated in order to further or protect the interests of the United States are embedded in your fabric. They're a part of you and you're a part of them. All of the operations you have accomplished and the people you used along the way...all of them are still a part of you. Beau, Reed, and the rest of them. That will never change. You were down and dirty with the best of them and there's a reason they called you the Eliminator. You were the best field agent we had and you walked away from it when Marcos was killed. I'm sorry for that, Trace, you know I am, but walking away from it didn't erase it from your life. Do I really have to explain this to you?"

"This line is not secure, Harry."

"To hell with it!" Harry snapped. "I don't care if it's secure or not. Now, do you want to hear this or not?"

"I don't."

"That's too bad because I'm going to tell you, anyway," he replied, calming. "Trace, Nevredev's daughter has become a powerful lord in her own right. Nathalia Nevredevova has worked hard to rise to power over the past couple of years to fill the void left by her father."

"Her father isn't dead," Trace interrupted quietly. "Hence, the botched assassination."

"I know," Harry said. "Her father's on life support in a hospital in Kiev, but his absence has left a hole at the top of their organization that Nathalia has worked hard to fill. Rumor has it she's gunning for you in revenge for what you did to her father."

Trace was quiet a moment, mulling over the information. More than anything, he simply felt depressed.

"They never knew my real name," he said softly. "They don't know anything about me."

"I know," Harry said. "But they know your face. They have spies all over the goddamn place. Bribery works wonders. If they really want to find out who you truly are, they can do it."

"You think they'll go that far?"

"I think they might," Harry said. "Maybe they're already on to you for all we know. Her father isn't doing so well. There's talk of pulling the plug. If that old man dies, half of the Ukrainian underground is going to be gunning for you."

"All of this happened over two years ago. Why now?"

"Nathalia never had the power until now," Harry replied. "The other generals in the organization didn't care about what you did to Nevredev because it gave them the opportunity to move into his spot. But now *she's* moved into his spot and she wants you dead. You *know* Nathalia, Trace. You used her to get to her old man. You know how she is."

Trace grunted softly, with regret, with some impatience. "So what do I do?"

"Go to the Ukraine and take out Nathalia."

"Is that my only choice?"

"It would solve the problem. There are a lot of people who would like to see her gone and would probably thank you for it."

Trace hung his head, eventually running a hand through his dirty hair in a laborious and thoughtful gesture. "What are my other options?"

"I'm going to suggest changing your name and moving to the Yukon."

"That's not going to happen."

"Then you need to be on your toes."

"You'll keep me posted?"

"You know I will," Harry said. Then, he paused. "Any chance I can get you here to D.C. for a full briefing?"

"If it looks like the threat is real, you can."

"I think it is. Can you make a trip out here next week?"

"I'll let you know."

Trace hung up. He didn't want to hear any more. He

just sat there for several long moments. He didn't even know what he was feeling other than disappointment. He ran a weary hand over his face; dear God, did it ever go away? The anxiety? The feeling of being hunted day and night? He thought he'd been doing so well at assimilating back to a normal life with his parents and brothers. He had a job that didn't require him to put bullets in people. He'd just met a woman that...

Kiki. Trace glanced quickly at the clock, seeing that he had little time to shower and get over to the restaurant. He thought of her beauty, her wit, her giggly charm. God, he just loved everything about her. He'd never felt like that in his life.

And now this.

Now he just felt sick.

Trace jumped into the shower, scrubbing down as his mind whirled with the news. When he should have been thinking of the threat against him, he could only think of Kiki. He wondered if she'd go to Washington with him. He would sure like her to. As he quickly shaved, he tried to think of a good story to give her as to why he had to go and why he wanted her to come. As he was thinking of her, the house, and her silly daughters, he thought of the incident that morning. He thought of the dead burglar in the bathroom doorway and...

And!

...it had been a white male. In that neighborhood, a white male was an anomaly. The demographic in that neighborhood was mostly Black and Hispanic. Trace paused as he rinsed off his face, thinking of the figure he'd seen. It had been a brief flash, as he hadn't really stopped to take a good look, but he distinctly remembered seeing a young, white male.

He rinsed off his face. The burglar had smashed the downstairs window to get in. It had been a sloppy entry. A professional...

...oh, God...a professional....

Paranoia gripped him. If he was the suspicious type, and he was, he might think that the break-in was no accident. Maybe Harry's call had come twelve hours too late. Maybe he was already being watched and, along with him, they were watching Kiki. Maybe the guy broke in to kidnap her or interrogate her, not rob her. Maybe he spoke with a Ukrainian accent. But he was dead so they'd never know.

He turned the shower off, thinking. He struggled not to be freaked out but it was difficult. All he could think of was getting out of Pasadena, like Harry had suggested, but he knew that wouldn't solve the problem. If he left, those in pursuit would go after his family and, possibly, after Kiki, trying to figure out where he had gone. No, running wasn't the answer. If the Ukrainians were already here, then Trace needed to be here to protect those he loved. If he had to take them all on, he would. And he would win. He wasn't going to let someone else he loved fall victim to that gang of thugs.

Especially Kiki.

· · ·

The log cabin-style restaurant that was a staple in Pasadena for fifty years was packed on this Friday night. Trace entered the dim restaurant with the sawdust all over the floor, his gaze searching out any familiar faces. Immediately, he spied Jesse standing with three women, but it was so crowded that he really couldn't get a good look at the women. As he drew closer, he could see that Jesse and the women were standing in a little group. Embry and Esme were partially facing him, while the third woman had her back to him. When Trace got a good look at the rear view of the third woman, he had to take a breath.

Kiki was clad in a stunning black dress, rather short, but it displayed the best legs he had ever seen. Her hair was long and silky and when she turned around to look at him, he was struck speechless for a moment. The dress was sexy without being slutty and she was absolutely a knockout in it.

He felt warm and giddy at the sight of her.

"Hey there," she said, smiling. "So you decided to join us?"

He grinned in return, realizing he very much wanted to kiss her. He settled for putting a casual hand on her back in greeting.

"Sorry I'm late," he said. "Time got away from me. Is everybody hungry?"

"Starving," Embry said. She had cleaned up well and was dressed in a skirt and cute blouse. "I've always loved this place."

"Then let's get a table and eat."

The girls rushed toward the hostess stand with Jesse close behind. It afforded Trace and Kiki a few moments of alone time and he leaned over and kissed her cheek.

"You look amazing," he said softly. "Have I told you lately how beautiful you are?"

She smiled modestly. "Not lately."

"Then I apologize. I'll make sure to tell you every single day."

He had her by the elbow as they were shown to a table. The place was a steakhouse and everyone had some kind of beef on their plate. Jesse, a divorced father with two small girls, took to Embry and Esme and spent the evening chatting it up with them while Trace and Kiki sat conspicuously close to each other, talking softly between them and, on occasion, joining in on Jesse and the girls' conversation.

They ate, they drank, and generally had a marvelous time. In fact, when it was over and the bill was paid, the girls bolted up and headed for the parking lot as the grown-ups moved a little more slowly.

"Well," Jesse said, as they stepped away from the table. "I usually charge five bucks an hour for babysitting but I'll waive my fee for tonight."

Trace had his hand on the small of Kiki's back as they headed out of the restaurant. "What are you talking about?" he asked.

Jesse cocked an eyebrow. "I'm talking about the fact that you two were out on a date while I watched the kids," he said. "Next time, you two go to dinner somewhere and I'll take the girls to a pizza place."

Kiki grinned. "It wasn't that bad."

Jesse snorted and rolled his eyes. "You two make a very cute couple."

He moved toward the front door, snorting ironically as Trace and Kiki watched him go. Trace looked at Kiki.

"He was mostly right," he said quietly. "I didn't want to share you."

Kiki was torn between remorse and not particularly caring. "He isn't mad, is he?"

Trace shook his head. "Of course not," he said. "But I'm going to be hearing about this for the next week."

They grinned at each other, knowingly and perhaps a bit coyly, as they exited the restaurant and headed out into the dark parking lot. Jesse and the girls were already at the cars, chatting softly under the mercury vapor lights.

Now came the part about heading home. Trace knew he would be going to Kiki's house tonight and her girls were there, so it seemed to him that somebody had better say something before he showed up and the girls had no idea why he was there. He glanced at Kiki as they approached the cars but she simply smiled at him, coyly, which set his heart to racing. He was rather interested in that coy look. But he was more interested in making sure Esme and Embry wouldn't be surprised when he showed up at their door and a thought occurred to him.

"Ladies," he said as they walked up to them. He crooked his finger at the girls. "A word, please?"

Curious, Esme and Embry went to him. Kiki tried to follow but he held out a hand, holding her off, as he took the girls a few feet away. Then he began speaking to them in a low voice as Kiki and Jesse stood by her car, watching the scene curiously.

"I wonder what he's saying to them," Kiki said. She glanced at Jesse. "He's not plotting against me, is he? Pulling them into his evil plans?"

Jesse laughed. "I wouldn't put anything past him," he said. "He's probably plotting a coup. He's been trained for that kind of thing, you know. Didn't he tell you he worked for the CIA?"

Kiki nodded, watching Trace as he muttered to her girls, who seemed to be taking whatever he was saying very seriously.

"He did," she said. "He said he was an analyst. We really didn't talk much about it, though."

Jesse's humorous demeanor faded. There was an odd gleam to his eye. "Is that what he told you?" he asked. "An analyst?"

Kiki caught on to his tone of voice and turned to look at him. "Yes," she said. "Why? That wasn't the truth?"

Jesse nodded quickly. "It's the truth," he conceded, his gaze drifting to his brother. "But...well, don't ever tell him that I mentioned it, but if you're going to get involved with him, then you should know that I personally think it was much more than that."

Kiki was very interested. "What more?"

Jesse shrugged. "I don't know," he said, now seemingly struggling for words. "Just...more. I've said too much already. Don't tell him I said anything, okay?"

Kiki shook her head. "I won't, but now you have me curious," she said. "Did he do something else for the CIA that he's not telling me about?"

Jesse shoved his hands into his pockets, giving a sigh. He'd started this conversation so he figured he should say what he'd meant in the first place. "Honestly, I really don't know," he said. "He was in D.C. for a lot of years, but there were times that he would just drop off the grid for months at a time. Personally, I don't think he was an analyst. I think he was in the field."

"Doing what?"

"What does the CIA usually do?"

"Spy?"

Jesse nodded as if she'd hit the nail on the head. "Spy," he agreed. "And other things. Assassinations and stuff. My brother is a crack shot. You've never seen anyone shoot as good as he can. And the way he thinks...maybe you've picked up on it, but he's two steps ahead of everyone else. Always. He plans things out to the last detail. That's what makes him so good at the construction game, too. He doesn't miss a thing. And sometimes...well, I know it's crazy to think this, but sometimes he just has this look on his face."

"What *kind* of look?"

"Like he's a hunter."

Kiki pondered that for a moment, moving her attention from Jesse back to Trace, who was now grinning at her children, who were giggling and nodding their heads. "I haven't seen that part of him yet," she said. "He just seems like a nice, normal guy to me."

"He is," Jesse said quickly. "But...oh, hell, I'm really going to get into trouble if he knows I've said all of this, but he had a hard time back East with his wife and all. I think that's why he came back to Pasadena, just to get away from that life he lived on the East Coast. I think meeting you was really fortuitous because he's seemed kind of lost and depressed for a long time. But since meeting you, he seems a lot happier. That means a lot to my family, just so you know. Even if you are Jimmy Wickham's little sister."

He meant it as a joke and Kiki grinned. But her gaze was still on Trace, who by now realized she was looking at him. He reached out and gently tapped Esme on the arm and said something, and both girls turned to see their mother looking at them. All three of them then approached her with various smirks on their faces. Kiki cocked an eyebrow at the group.

"You all look like the cat that has swallowed the canary," she said. "Why the goofy expressions? What world-domination plan have you been cooking up?"

In reply, Esme reached out and put her arm around her mother, pulling her towards the car. "Come on, Mom," she said. "Let's head home. We have to talk to you."

Kiki looked over her shoulder at Trace, who simply smiled and waved at her. He didn't seem to have much to say, or even really try to bid her a private goodbye, so Kiki let her daughters drag her across the parking lot as she called back to their two dinner companions.

"See you guys later," she said. "Thanks for dinner!"

Trace waved at her again, as did Jesse. That was the last thing Kiki saw before Esme was forcing her into her car. Snickering at her pushy daughters, she fired up the engine as the girls jumped into the car and slammed the doors. Putting the car in gear, she backed out and pulled away from the parking lot while Trace and Jesse still stood there, watching her go. Once she pulled out onto the street and headed for the freeway, she turned to Embry, in the front seat.

"Okay," she said suspiciously. "What was that all about? Why the bum's rush to the car?"

Embry grinned. "Because we had to talk to you," she said. "Mr. Rocklin asked us to do it in private. He said this should come from us."

The light turned red and Kiki brought the car to a stop, looking at her daughters expectantly. "What should come from you?"

Embry and Esme looked at each other before Embry continued. "Mr. Rocklin is really concerned about you living in that house," she said. "He said that he asked you if he could move in and rent a room from you as a tenant but that you were concerned about what Es and I would think. He said you didn't want to do anything inappropriate in front of us."

Kiki was rather surprised that Trace had brought that up to the girls. He had been clear that he would let her handle her children when it came to their relationship so this came as something of a shock. She wasn't so sure she liked it, in fact.

"I told you that earlier today," she said. "You two weren't hot on the idea, remember? You told me it wasn't a good idea to shack up with a guy I'd only known three days."

Embry put her hand on her mom's arm. "I know we did," she said. "But this was different, Mom. He asked our permission, if he could move in with you, you know, to protect you and all. I know we said it wasn't a good idea for him to move in with you, but he seems really concerned about you. I believe him when he says that he just wants to make sure you're safe and I'm really glad you've found someone who cares about you like that. He wanted our permission because he thought Es and I should be the ones to really make the decision if we were okay with it or not. After talking to him, I have to say that I've changed my mind."

Kiki didn't know what to say. She looked between her girls, reinforcing the fact that her daughters were really all grown up. They were logical, well-adjusted women and she was coming to understand now why Trace had approached them. It wasn't that he needed their permission but it was clear he wanted their approval. He was serious about protecting their mother and wasn't going to wait on something that had to do with her safety. He was including the girls in something that would, realistically, affect them all. So what if he hadn't let her handle it; as far as she was concerned, it had been the right way to do it.

Kiki was still treating her girls like fragile children and he wasn't.

"I didn't tell him what you both said earlier about him moving in with me," she finally said. "He didn't know you didn't think it was a good idea."

The light turned green and Kiki drove on. Both girls were watching their mother as she navigated Rosemead Boulevard. "He didn't say he'd talked to you about it or anything," Esme said from the back seat. "He just explained to us that he felt it was safer if he moved in considering what had happened. He told us that he thinks you're pretty special and it would kill him if anything happened to you. I think he's a good guy, Mom. I can't think badly about someone who clearly likes you so much and is trying so hard to help you."

A smile crossed Kiki's lips. "So you're okay with it, then? Him renting a room from me, I mean."

The girls both nodded. "I like him," Embry said. "And the way he looked at you at dinner...not even Dad did that. Mr. Rocklin really likes you, Mom."

Kiki could feel herself blushing, struggling not to grin like an idiot as the freeway on-ramp loomed. "I really like him, too," she said softly. "Thanks, ladies...well, thanks for being so understanding."

"So you'll let him move in?"

"I will."

Embry looked at her sister. "We are going to have *such* a hot stepdad!"

As the girls broke into laughter, Kiki rolled her eyes. "He's not your stepdad yet."

"He will be!" Embry crowed.

Kiki didn't say anything, too embarrassed and giddy to get into that kind of conversation with them at this point. She listened to her girls giggle and chatter about how cute Trace was and how they were going to have all of their sorority friends over to the house to drool all over him.

Kiki simply shook her head and kept her mouth shut, listening to her daughters grow more ridiculous and silly by the minute. But it was good to hear, a joy in their voices that she hadn't heard in a very long time. The death of Mark had taken a lot of joy out of them and it was good to hear that it was returning.

Trace, she knew, had a lot to do with it. He was making them all feel like life, for them, was going on, that there were good things out there in the world for them.

For Kiki.

Maybe the relationship wouldn't go anywhere. Maybe it would. Maybe he would be their stepdad someday. But in any case, in some small way, Trace Rocklin was helping the entire family heal from something that had been devastating and shocking.

Although Kiki hadn't known it at the time, the day he'd given her that terrible estimate on restoring her beast of a house had been the day her life had changed forever.

TWELVE
TWO WEEKS LATER

TRACE SAT in his office at Rocklin Construction, looking over the landscape architect's plans for Kiki's yard. That included the renovation of the antique fountain in front, the one she was so determined to restore as the highlight of the yard. Big and heavy, the fountain itself was some kind of architectural masterpiece that the landscape architect was in love with almost as much as Kiki was.

The young, highly educated Hispanic man, who had done a lot of work for Rocklin in the past, had taken a million pictures of the thing on the day he showed up to walk the property and when he came back the next day, he'd brought some guy who was an expert in antique fountains with a background in art history. The older man with the buzz cut and big, round glasses had praised the fountain's design before carefully inspecting the piece.

As Trace and Kiki had watched with great curiosity, the fountain expert had crawled all around the fountain and even got into it at one point, inspecting the underbelly of the part that actually spilled the water forth, and declared that it was from the turn-of-the-last-century French designer by the name of Henri de la Mere. It was cast iron encased in a type of clay that, when fired, gave it a very hard and timeless finish. It was evidently a patented process and the expert gave a great explanation on how it was done and why the fountain was so valuable.

In fact, he offered to buy it from Kiki for twenty thousand dollars in cash but she politely refused, saying that the house wouldn't be complete without its fountain. The art designer agreed but told her that he would be the first one to buy it should she change her mind. Kiki assured him that she never would, so the expert and the landscape designer got together to figure out a way to restore the fountain to full working order as part of the entire landscape redesign process.

So the process of restoring the house went on with Trace as a very big part of it. A little over two weeks after meeting the beautiful Kiki Wickham Conrad, he felt as if he'd known her forever. He felt as if they'd always been together, just the two of them, the farting dog, and her giggly daughters who had returned to college twelve days ago. But those three days he'd spent with the girls and their mother had been amazing days.

After getting the girls' permission to move in with their mother, Trace had his own bedroom in the house, right across the hall from Kiki's, and she was the first thing he saw in the morning and the last thing he saw at night. She had dinner waiting for him nightly and he called her several times throughout the day simply to hear her voice. It was the fastest relationship he'd ever been a part of but nothing in his life had ever felt so right. Everything about it was meant to be as far as he was concerned. He felt as if he were walking on air, every day, and he'd never felt like that in his life. Giddy was a good word for it.

He was in love.

He hadn't told her that yet, though. It never seemed to be the right time. Telling a woman he loved her after not even knowing her three weeks seemed like rushing things a bit, but his heart told him otherwise. Was there even a time frame on love? Trace had been in love, once, a long time ago when he'd first met his ex-wife, but that seemed like a lifetime ago. He couldn't even remember that time, really. All he knew was that, here and now, was the best time of his life. He'd never been happier.

"Hey, Trace."

His brother, Shaun, was standing in the doorway. Big and blond, Sean was the middle brother and by far the most genius of the group. Snapped from thoughts of Kiki, Trace rocked back in his office chair.

"Shaun," he greeted. "What can I do for you?"

Shaun came into Trace's office, papers in his hand. "Did you see that Andre Mercado is billing us for the art historian's fee on the Conrad job?" he asked.

Trace shook his head. "I didn't," he replied. "But I was there when the guy came out to inspect the antique fountain. He helped Mercado get it up and running. As of yesterday, water was flowing through it once again. It's really something to see. Mercado has water lilies in it and other aquatic plants. It's gorgeous."

Shaun grunted, looking at the invoice in his hand. "It should be at that price," he said. "Ten thousand dollars for that guy to come out and tell you it was a French-designed fountain?"

Trace grinned. "It was worth it," he said. "A French-designed fountain designed to look like an old Spanish water feature so it's in tune with the architecture of the house. The restoration needed to be done by an expert."

Shaun looked up from the paper, eyeing his brother. He knew, as did the rest of the family and the office in general, that Trace was living at Kiki Conrad's big house over on Raymond in Pasadena. Trace's official story for the first week was that he was simply helping out an old friend but it soon became very clear that it was far more than that. Kiki had even come to their offices, twice, to go to lunch with him and everyone had gotten a look at the woman that had Trace so enamored. The receptionist was very jealous and even went into the bathroom to cry about it, but everyone else had been very nice to Kiki. Especially Jesse and Shaun. Anyone who had Trace's heart was worth their respect. They couldn't have been happier for their brother.

Rick Rocklin, however, was another story. Although very happy for his son, he had an element of reserve that no one else seemed to, unusual for the senior Rocklin. A softy for a beautiful woman, he was, nonetheless, rather reserved about his reaction to Trace moving into her house. Trace had even confronted his father about a week after he'd moved in and, over Jack Daniel's Honey Whiskey and Coke, they'd hashed out the fact that Rick was simply concerned for his eldest son, concerned that the man was going to end up getting hurt again just as he'd been hurt when his first wife had left him.

Two weeks later, Trace was still trying to convince his father that he and Kiki were the real deal. Jesse, and Shaun to a certain extent, was still trying to convince the old man as well.

Anything that made Trace so happy couldn't be all bad.

"Well," Shaun finally said. "It's your call, but just know that Mercado is already charging for this guy's services. Is he done with the job?"

Trace nodded. "The fountain is running fine," he said. "The guy replaced the inner workings, which ran on a kind of water-weight and pulley system, with electrical innards. I'm sure the fountain has never flowed as well as it does now. Kiki is happy and that's all that matters."

"Can I pay him?"

"You can."

Shaun nodded. "You know that this job is well over what you estimated, right?" he asked. "Is Kiki okay with that?"

Trace cleared his throat softly, looking somewhat awkward now. "No," he said, lowering his voice. "She doesn't know. I haven't told her because I'm going to cover the increase personally, so don't worry about it. And don't tell her if she calls to talk about invoices, okay?"

Shaun frowned. "You're covering the increase?"

"That's what I said."

"But that's at least forty thousand dollars by now."

"Get out of here. I've got work to do."

Shaun simply shook his head and headed out of the office. It was clear that Trace didn't want to talk about it, but it didn't make any sense to him that his brother would pay for renovations on a house he didn't even own. As Shaun passed down the hall, the receptionist walked by him, heading into Trace's office. She knocked softly on the doorjamb.

"Trace?" she said. "There's someone here to see you."

Trace, who had just turned to his computer, looked over his shoulder at the very young receptionist who'd had a crush on him since she had started working there six months ago. "Who is it?" he asked.

The receptionist leaned into the doorway, hoping he was noticing her cleavage. "He says he's an old friend," she said. "Harry King?"

Trace stared at her as the name sank in. *Harry King? God, that couldn't be a good thing, not at all. Harry King arriving unannounced? Cross-country no less?* Shocked, Trace stood up so quickly that he knocked a file folder off of his desk, scattering papers. But he didn't notice because he was charging out of his office, heading for reception.

"Where is he?" he demanded. "Up front?"

The receptionist nodded, wondering why Trace

suddenly looked so edgy. "Yes," she replied as he stormed away from her. "He's at my desk. I'll pick up your papers!"

The last few words were shouted after him, but Trace didn't acknowledge her. He kept walking, down the hall with the glass-walled offices, past Shaun and Jesse and his father, past the project manager's bullpen, before emerging into the modestly decorated reception area.

Immediately, he saw a tall, good-looking Black man standing near the front desk, inspecting a model of one of Rocklin's former projects. Startled anew to see Harry King standing there, Trace walked right up to the man.

"Harry?" he said, incredulous. "What in the hell are you doing here?"

Harry turned on Trace, his face lighting up with a megawatt smile. Harry had the whitest teeth Trace had ever seen. He extended his hand in greeting.

"God, you look terrible," he said to Trace as the man shook his hand. "Living in California does nothing for you. You need to go back home."

Trace couldn't help but grin as Harry squeezed his hand. "This *is* my home," he said. "So answer my question - what are you doing here? Are you on vacation?"

Harry let go of his hand. "No, no vacation," he said, the smile on his face fading as he looked at Trace. "Do you have a minute?"

The bottom dropped out of Trace's stomach. He knew, instinctively, that the coming conversation could not be a good thing. After his phone call with Harry two weeks ago, he was more than concerned to see the man here at his place of business. In fact, Harry was the only person who knew where Trace was because that's the way he wanted it. Out of necessity for Trace's former line of work, that's the way it had to be. Now, he was growing nervous.

"Sure," Trace said. "Let's take a walk out in the parking lot. I'll show you the building. It's brand-new, you know. We just built it about a year ago."

Harry had an odd look on his face. "How about we go into your office," he said quietly. "Does it face the street?"

"It does."

"Do you have a conference room or another room that doesn't?"

Now, Trace was becoming very concerned. "Sure," he said. "Come with me."

Trace led Harry back down the hallway, introducing the man to his father and brothers as he went. They were all very happy to meet Harry and a few minutes of pleasant conversation ensued, but all the while, Trace was nearly crazy with the need to get the man alone. He'd come a very long way for a protected and private conversation and as Harry and Rick chatted, Trace's mind wandered to the possibilities. He knew it had to do with Nathalia Nevredevova. There was nothing else it could be. But *what* did it have to do with her? Had something happened to her? Or to her father?

Trace couldn't wait any longer to know. He had to break Harry away from his dad because he knew that Rick would talk the man's ear off. Trace led Harry down to the end of the hall, took a right, and ended up in a small, executive conference room that was windowless. Shutting the door behind him, he faced Harry.

"What in the hell is going on?" he asked, his voice low. "Why the preventative protocols?"

Harry eyed Trace as he took a seat. He sighed heavily. "I had to come," he said. "There are things you need to know and a phone call wasn't an option. In case I was followed, I don't want to be near a window or wall by the street. Sit down, Trace. We need to talk."

Trace did as he was told, facing Harry over the Cherrywood conference table. "What's happened?"

Harry sighed again as if unsure where to begin. "That conversation we had a couple of weeks ago about Nathalia," he said. "Things have escalated, unfortunately. I told you I'd keep you posted so here it is—Nathalia Nevredevova is now in charge of her father's conglomerate. Nevredev died two days ago in Kiev and our sources tell us that Nathalia is out for your blood. In fact, our contacts think she has known where you are for a while. They think she's already sent men after you."

Oddly, Trace seemed to grow calm. At least now he knew and he wasn't surprised by it. He shifted into professional mode in an instant, back in the game now, back in the fight for his life, in the fight between good and evil. He had that ability to shift focus like that but it had taken years of practice.

He was back in his element.

"After our conversation a couple of weeks ago, I agree

with you," he said. "There was something I didn't tell you at that time."

Harry was interested. "Did something happen?"

Trace leaned back in his chair thoughtfully. "To make a long story short, I started dating a woman a couple of weeks ago," he said. "I hadn't known her two days when someone broke into her house and tried to kill her. Understand that she lives on the west side of Pasadena, which is predominately Hispanic and Black. The man who broke in was young and very white. That's the only glimpse I got of him, but in that neighborhood, that was an oddity. A random white guy breaking into a house in a minority neighborhood makes no sense at all."

Harry grew serious. "Do you really think they were trying to kill her? Or trying to gain information from her?"

Trace shrugged. "We'll never know," he said. "She killed the guy by stabbing him through the eye with a pair of scissors."

Harry flinched at the visual that statement provoked. "But you think it might have been a Nevredevova operative looking for you?"

Trace nodded. "It's possible they've been watching me," he said. "On the premise that they have, they knew enough that I'd been seeing her for a very short amount of time but it was enough so that they broke into her house. I can't prove it, of course, but it makes perfect sense."

"Has anything happened since?"

Trace shook his head. "No," he replied. "It's been quiet, mostly because if they are really watching me, they probably assumed I personally killed the guy and they're not going to make another attempt so soon, at least not until they have reinforcements."

"It could have been a lone operative."

Again, Trace shook his head. "That's not how Nathalia works," he said flatly. "She sends her people into situations in groups of two or three. I'm willing to bet there's at least one or two more around here, watching me as we speak."

"If you really believe that, then you probably shouldn't leave your girlfriend alone if they're watching her house," Harry said. "If they tried once to get to her, they'll try again."

Trace lifted his eyebrows. "She's not alone," he said. "Her house is under construction, a massive renovation project, so there are people there all of the time. Nathalia wouldn't risk doing anything with witnesses around, so Kiki is safe for now. She's never alone. I make sure of that."

"Kiki?"

A grin flickered on his lips. "The name of my future wife," he said quietly. "Kiki Conrad. You'll like her, Harry. She's...well, she's amazing. I can't describe her any better than that. You'll just have to meet her."

Harry didn't move to congratulate him. In fact, his mood seemed to dampen. "Trace," he said slowly, shaking his head. "If Nathalia's people really are here, as the evidence seems to suggest, then you need to get out of here. They've found you, my friend. Somehow, someway, they've found you and they are going to try and kill you. Do you want your girlfriend to end up collateral damage?"

Trace's smile turned into something of a grimace. "That's not going to happen."

"You can't know that."

Now, Trace was starting to get defensive. "Yes, I can," he said. "And here's how—you will make it known, through our contacts, that if any of Nathalia's men come near me or her, or anyone associated with me or her, I will unleash hell on earth like they've never seen. I have that capability and you know it. I'll wipe out her and her entire damn family, Harry. I'll wipe out anyone who has even looked at her. I will go on the offensive if I have to and that's not something they'll want to deal with."

Harry saw, in that speech, a flash of the man he'd known for years, an assassin so highly trained that he could take out anyone, anywhere, like they never existed. Trace Rocklin had been a man of such talents until he'd walked away from it. Or, at least tried to walk away from it. But men like Trace were never completely free of the chaos they were involved in. They were part of the very fabric of it.

"The Eliminator," he muttered, satisfaction in his tone. "Welcome back, man. We've missed you."

Trace simply looked at him, something deadly brewing in those hazel eyes. "You'll make it known, then."

"I'll do what I can," Harry agreed. "But you know what I'm going to say, don't you? The only way this will end is if you go to the Ukraine and remove Nathalia yourself. There is no other choice in this, Trace. If you ever want peace in your life, if you really want to marry your Kiki and live happily ever after, then you're going to have to do one last job to make sure you can. If you don't, you'll be looking over your shoulder for the rest of your life. And you know that Nathalia would take a lot of pleasure in killing a woman you loved."

That caused Trace to stiffen. Nothing else Harry had said made an impact on him but mentioning Kiki and Nathalia in the same breath did something to him. His jaw tightened and began to tick, the expression on his face nothing short of murderous.

"Then you'd better make sure she gets the message," he growled. "Any move against me or people around me, no matter how small, and everyone dies."

"That's the gist of it?"

"That's the gist of it."

Harry considered his options at that point. Trace seemed to think that threatening Nathalia would be enough. But he knew, deep down, that Trace knew differently. He knew a simple threat wasn't going to mean anything in the end. There had to be more than that; much more.

"I can't get that message flowing through the channels any time soon," Harry said. "You know that. Stuff like that takes time. Meanwhile, if she's got people on you, they're still going to do whatever it takes to get to you. They could be watching your office for all you know. What happens if they try to take out your dad or your brothers? Do you realize that by staying here, you risk them all? You're not that careless, man. Do I really have to explain this game to you, Trace? You know what you have to do. How many times do I have to say it?"

Trace inhaled; long and deep and thoughtful. He didn't want to hear this, any of it, but he had no choice. He was resisting his role in this situation and they both knew it. More than that, he knew that what Harry said was true. He knew why Harry had come and it wasn't to put him in a position he didn't want to be in. It wasn't to put him back in the game he had walked away from. It was to help him. Finally, Trace sat forward and put his face in his hands.

"Damn," he groaned. "Damn it all to hell."

Harry could see that he was finally understanding the reality of the situation, the truth of what needed to happen. To be honest, he was very relieved. He put a hand on Trace's shoulder.

"I know, man," he said sympathetically. "I know. But that's why I came to see you personally. If you ever want to be free of the shadow of death, you're going to have to go into the field one last time. You're going to have to kill Nathalia."

Trace just sat there with his hands on his face. "Do you have any idea what it means to be really happy, Harry?" he asked, his voice muffled by his hands over his mouth. "Well, I didn't. I really didn't know at all until I met Kiki. I'm living with her, you know. We're renovating that big behemoth of a house she bought because she wants to turn it into a bed and breakfast. She wants us to live there and be a host to this fantasy world like that guy who ran Fantasy Island. People will come to our location, happy, and leave happier. All Kiki wants is joy and peace and I want it with her. We're damn happy, Harry. I don't want to leave that world, not to go back into hell."

Harry was sympathetic. "If you don't go to hell, hell will come to you," he said quietly. "Is that what you want?"

Trace took his hands away from his face and sat back in his chair. "No," he said. "It's not. The world Kiki and I live in...it's heaven, Harry. I don't want that jeopardized for anything."

Harry reached into the pocked of his suit jacket and pulled forth an envelope, handing it over to Trace. Trace looked at it for a moment before opening it up. It was a first class plane ticket, departing Los Angeles International Airport tomorrow evening for Washington Dulles.

"You need to come back for a briefing before you head over to the Ukraine," he said quietly. "I'll be on that plane with you tomorrow when you head back. You need to understand the dynamics of Nathalia's cartel now. We'll brief you on the details before you go."

Trace just stared at the ticket. It was all happening whether or not he wanted it to, but he realized as he looked at the ticket that he wanted it to happen. He wanted to take care of those who would threaten him and the world of joy and passion he'd had a taste of. He'd never known anything like it and he couldn't let his past take away his future. As reluctant as he was to go, to leave Kiki, he knew he had to go.

He had no choice.

"Okay," he said, closing up the envelope. "Let me wrap

up things here and I'll be on the plane tomorrow. Do you want to come over tonight and meet Kiki? I'd like you to, Harry. She's the only reason I'm doing this. If she wasn't involved, I wouldn't be going at all, but you're right—Nathalia would do a victory dance if she took out the woman I love. I can't let that happen while there's still breath in my body."

Harry nodded. "Sure," he said. "I'd like to meet the woman who finally caught your eye. I didn't think you had it in you, to be honest."

Trace smiled weakly. "When you see her, you'll get it."

Harry's gaze lingered at him. "Seeing your expression when you talk about her, I get it already."

There was nothing more to say. Harry stood up, as did Trace, each of them knowing what they had to do, knowing what was coming. It was like old times again, only these old times weren't good times. They were times of necessity.

Necessity to save the free world.

Trace's world.

"I'm going to the Los Angeles office for a while," Harry said as they headed for the door. "I'll come over later tonight if that's all right. Text me the address."

Trace nodded. "I will," he said. "It'll give me time to break the news to her that I'm going to be gone for a while. I may have Jesse go stay with her, just to make sure she's not alone."

Harry opened the conference room door. "Are you sure you want her staying there at all, Trace?" he said softly. "If Nathalia's people are watching the house...."

Trace put up a hand. "If they're watching it, then they'll see me leave," he said. "It's me they want, not her. If they see I've left, then it'll take the focus off of her. Besides, like I said, with all of the activity going on at the house, they're not going to chance doing anything."

Harry shrugged; he didn't particularly agree with him. "They might try to use her to get to you," he said. "It sounds like they tried it once."

Trace knew that; he was trying to talk himself into believing that if he left, the problem would be solved. But he knew it wasn't that easy. "I'm going to have to let Jesse in on this if I ask him to stay at the house with her," he said. "That ought to thrill him. My brother has always accused me of being a spy. Now he'll know he was right all along, the little shit."

Harry grinned. "I've got a brother like that," he said. Then, his smile faded. "If he does stay there, make sure he's armed."

"To the teeth."

There wasn't much more to say at that point. The path was set and they knew what needed to be done. Reluctantly, but it needed to be done, nonetheless.

Trace walked Harry to the door and shook the man's hand, watching him as he headed out into the parking lot beyond. Then, he turned around and headed back into the offices, seeking out his father specifically and, seeing the man alone, went into his office and shut the door.

It was a very long and somewhat emotional conversation he had with his father where Trace informed him that he would be taking a hiatus from his job for an unknown length of time. When Trace was finished with Rick, he sought out Jesse, who was just getting ready to leave for the day. He and his brother had another very interesting conversation, during which a lot of Jesse's suspicions of his brother's real role with the CIA were clarified.

The first time Jesse said *I knew it!*, Trace punched his brother in the gut.

Little shit!

THIRTEEN

THE HOUSE SMELLED like fried chicken, filling the air with that savory odor that had Stanley underfoot as Kiki moved around the kitchen. The dog was hungry so she ended up feeding him some kibble as she finished up the chicken.

There was a ton of renovation going on in the house at this point but the kitchen was one of the last frontiers to be touched, so Kiki still had a full kitchen to work with. It was a good thing, too, because Trace not only liked to eat, he liked to cook as well, so they spent their nights making dinner and having drinks. Kiki's pants were starting to feel tight because of it.

She had to laugh at herself, the woman who never let herself gain any weight because, in the past, Mark would make comments if she did. Trace, however, didn't care in the least. On the weekends, he liked to cook for her and he liked to see her eat. It had become a routine for them—

they'd stuff themselves at dinner time and then he'd take her outside and make her go for a long walk along Mountain Street, across Fair Oaks, and into residential neighborhoods until they made about a two-mile loop.

They always brought Stanley along on their walks but the dog had little stamina so Trace would end up carrying the pooch most of the walk. He and Stanley had formed quite a bond because of it. But it was lovely, and domestic, and just about as wonderful as Kiki had ever imagined a relationship to be.

She'd never known anything so utterly wonderful.

So, she cooked for Trace on a regular basis and she also washed his clothes, made his bed, and bought him little things that struck her fancy. Trace came home to her every night and that's the way she loved it. Nearly every night after their walk, they would kiss and cuddle, watching television in Kiki's bedroom, and it was all quite wonderful. But they still hadn't sealed the deal yet with sex.

Heavy petting and lots of touching, but no sex. Trace seemed to pull back before things got too heavy and when Kiki questioned him about it, he said, simply, that he hadn't moved into her house to get her into bed. Having known her only three weeks, he didn't want to move too fast and ruin anything. Kiki understood for the most part but it was getting to the point where she didn't much care. She wanted the man in her bed no matter how long they'd known each other. To her, it just seemed like the natural progression of their relationship.

So her wicked plan was to cook him a decadent dinner

this evening and take advantage of him when he was too overcome by food to fight her off. She'd gotten a recipe for fried chicken and waffles from a cooking show, which included bacon-infused maple syrup, and she was in the process of finishing up the chicken when she heard Trace's truck pull up in the driveway. It made her heart leap with excitement to hear it. Then she heard the truck door slam just as she was taking the chicken out of a cast iron skillet, putting it on brown paper bags to cool off and drain extra grease.

Keys in the back door. As soon as Trace opened the door and entered, he grunted happily.

"Good Lord, woman," he said. "It smells like heaven in this house right now. What are you making me for dinner?"

Kiki grinned as he tossed his keys on the counter and came up behind her, slipping his big arms around her and kissing her on the neck.

"Fried chicken, waffles, and bacon maple syrup," she said. "Everything you shouldn't be eating."

He held her tightly, his mouth still on her neck. "I don't give a damn," he muttered. "It smells like something I need to put in my mouth right this second. God, I'm lucky to have you."

She was trying to move to the waffle iron to make the waffles now that he was home, but he had such a grip on her that she couldn't move. And his mouth on her neck was making her body quiver. Before she realized it, she had turned in his arms, latching her mouth onto his, and he pulled her against him with such force that she grunted.

Trace was a very strong man, made apparent by the way he suddenly picked Kiki up and manhandled her onto the moveable island in the middle of the kitchen. They had purchased it from a furniture store to give her more counter space in the old kitchen, but the moment he put her on it, the wheels rolled and she nearly fell off. That brought out the laughter and the frenzied lust of the moment was broken.

"Tell me it's always going to be like this with us," Kiki said softly, her hands on his face. "Tell me you're always going to want to put me on the kitchen counter and take advantage of me."

He held her close, his forehead against hers, her legs wrapped around his hips where she still sat on the island. *Tell me it's always going to be like this with us.* He'd come home planning to tell her what had happened with Harry the very first thing, or at least as much as he could tell her, but as he held her in his arms and gently kissed her face, somehow, he just didn't want to do it at this moment. He wanted just a few more minutes of normalcy and laughter, of pretending that the future, for them, would always be full of rolling islands and passion.

Not full of killing people that were trying to kill him.

"It will always be like this, I promise," he said. "At least as far as I'm concerned. I've worked too hard to get where I am with you to let any of this change. I like it just the way it is."

She grinned and he kissed her one last time before setting her down on the floor. But the fact that she had been all wrapped up around his hips in a lovemaking position had him fairly aroused, so he tried to make himself more comfortable as Kiki went over to the waffle iron and poured in the batter.

Kiki couldn't help but notice he was spending an inordinate amount of time adjusting himself through his jeans and she fought off a smirk.

"We can take care of that, you know," she said as she closed the top of the waffle iron.

He wasn't sure what she meant. "What?" he asked, but when she turned and looked straight at his crotch, he laughed softly. "Oh, *that*. Well, let's eat first and then we'll talk about it."

Kiki moved over to get the plates out of the cabinet. "That's all we ever do, Trace. Talk about it. I'd like to see a little action one of these days."

He watched her as she pulled the plates down and began dishing out the fried chicken. "You can have as much action as you want, baby," he said. "I told you that I didn't move in here to get in your bed. I don't want you to think that my ultimate evil plans are being realized if we sleep together. I was trying to give you time to get adjusted to all of this before we progressed like that."

She turned to look at him, wryly. "What about *my* ultimate evil plans?" she wanted to know. "What if that was the only reason I let you move in here?"

He couldn't help but chuckle. "Was it?"

She kept a straight face. "Yes."

His laughter grew. "Okay, then," he said. "I wouldn't want to disappoint you."

She remained serious. "You *do* find me sexually attractive, don't you? I mean, it's not because you have some aversion to me, is it? Because if that's the problem, then we really need to talk about it."

His laughter vanished. In three strides he was on her, pulling her into his arms and kissing her so forcefully that she could hardly breathe. It was deep, hot, and delicious, and the lust that so easily sparked between them roared to life. But Trace stopped short of grabbing her breast or any other body part; he simply held her tightly as his lips did the talking for him. He could hear her gasp.

"You are, by far, the sexiest woman I have ever known," he muttered against her mouth. "I don't want to hear anything like that from you ever again. I would have screwed your brains out nightly since the day I met you if I thought I could get away with it, so my attraction to you has nothing to do with my holding off on the sex part of our relationship. Got that?"

Breathless, she nodded. "Got it."

His eyes drilled into her. "Good," he said. "Now, let's eat and then after we eat, you and I are going to pick up right here, right where we left off. Okay?"

He meant the kissing. She grinned. "Okay."

He let her go, watching her stagger because he had overwhelmed her so much with the force of his passion. Smiling, he went to the refrigerator and pulled out a bottle of white wine they kept in there. Stanley, finished with his kibble, came out of his doggy bed and came over to the refrigerator, begging for more food. Trace gave the dog a piece of cheese, knowing it would make him fart like crazy but he couldn't deny the pleading doggy eyes. He was very fond of Bullfrog. As Kiki finished up with the waffles and Stanley ate his cheese, Trace poured the wine.

"So I invited an old friend of mine over tonight after dinner," he said. "I hope that's okay. I really want you to meet him and he's only in town tonight."

Kiki had the waffles and chicken on the plates, drizzling both with the bacon syrup. "Of course it's okay," she said. "Who is it?"

He took a sip of his wine as he headed over to the little breakfast table they had in the kitchen. Stanley followed close on his heels, hoping for more food. "His name is Harry King," Trace said. "I've known him for twenty years. He and I worked together in Washington."

Kiki picked up the plates and headed to the table. "Oh?" she said. "Was he with the CIA, too?"

He nodded as he sat down, faced with an utterly delicious plate of food. "Yes," he replied. "Christ, this looks good. You are one amazing woman."

He reached out and took her hand, kissing it, as she sat down next to him. Then he picked up his knife and fork and plowed into the feast. Kiki was a little slower to eat. Mostly, she just liked to watch him and how happy he was when he ate her cooking. She loved watching *him*.

"I think I need to cut back on making big, heavy meals

like this," she said, taking a sip of her wine. "If we keep eating like this we're both going to weigh five hundred pounds before we realize it. It's just that I've never been able to cook like this before and it's really fun."

He nodded, mouth full. "Fun and delicious," he said. "You're a fabulous cook."

She grunted. "Thanks," she said. "All Mark liked to eat was fish or chicken and vegetables, so that's all I ever made."

Trace made a face. "Boring," he said. "I think one or two meals a week like this aren't going to kill us. It's been the best time of my life, bonding with you over greasy food."

Kiki laughed as she dug into her chicken. "Me, too," she said. "Who knew I could fall in love over mashed potatoes and steak?"

He stopped chewing, immediately looking at her. "Have you?" he said, swallowing the very big bite in his mouth. He was looking at her with a rather startled expression. "Fallen in love, I mean? Have you?"

She looked at him, rather coyly. "Have *you*?"

"I asked you first."

Kiki held his gaze for a moment before looking away, back to her food. "Would it scare you away if I told you that I had?"

"It would make me the happiest man on earth."

She looked up from her food, into his handsome face. There was so much joy and love in her heart that she was nearly bursting with it. What was not to love about the man? At that point, she almost couldn't remember when she hadn't loved him.

"You have made me happier than I've ever been in my life," she said softly. "The way you and I have bonded...it was like it was meant to be, Trace. I needed you and I think you needed me, and it's like the universe put us together at the right place and time. Everything about us has just meshed so well. I woke up the other day thinking that I have loved you since the start. You're everything worth loving."

He just stared at her. Kiki thought that his eyes actually grew moist. Reaching out, he pulled her out of her seat and onto his lap, and once she settled on his thighs, he put his arms around her so tightly that he was nearly squeezing the breath out of her. His face was in her bosom as he spoke.

"I have waited my entire life to hear that," he said, muffled. "I've known that I loved you since the beginning but I was too afraid to tell you, too afraid it would scare you off. If that happened, I don't know what I'd do. I never want to be without you, Kiki."

She smiled, her arms around his neck and her chin resting on the top of his head. "You won't be."

"Swear it?"

"Of course I do."

He was quiet for a moment, his hot breath against her cleavage. Love had been declared between them and, at that moment, things changed. Something had been cemented and that bond between them, the one Kiki had talked about, turned to steel. There was no turning back now.

"Will you marry me?" he asked softly.

It was the perfect moment for it, the perfect timing of a question that had been silently lingering between them since nearly the beginning. Tears sprang to her eyes at the beauty of the question.

"Of course I will," she murmured.

He squeezed her tighter. "Thank you," he whispered. "For everything...just...thank you."

Kiki thought he sounded rather emotional but she was emotional herself, so she simply sat there and held him, thinking that the future had never looked brighter. There wasn't anything about her life that wasn't perfect at the moment and she was more grateful than she could express.

Trace was grateful, too. To have her love was everything he'd ever dreamed of. But he was also deeply torn about what was coming and what he needed to tell her. It had been rather unfair of him to ask her to marry him before telling her something that could quite possibly change both of their lives forever, but he was feeling particularly selfish. He wanted her and he wanted to have something waiting for him when he returned from what was to be, inarguably, the most important mission of his life.

In a sense, he was doing all of this for Kiki because he couldn't bear the thought of his past bleeding onto her, affecting her, creating havoc for an innocent woman who just happened to fall in love with a former CIA operative. What he had to do was for her as well as for him.

He had to save them both.

And she needed to know that.

"How big of a ring do you want?" he asked, although his mind was still on the things he needed to talk to her about. He just wasn't sure how to start that part of the conversation.

Unaware of his turmoil, Kiki gently stroked his hair. "Giant."

"*How* giant?"

She giggled. "I'm just kidding," she said. "I don't need a rock. I just need you."

He kissed the flesh that was next to his mouth. "You've got me, forever," he said. "But I want to get you the ring you want, so maybe you can show me some pictures sometime."

She loosened up on his neck a bit so she could look at him. "I'll do better than that," she said. "We'll go out to the Santa Anita mall this weekend and I'll show you what I like. But I don't see any rush, do you? I think if you give me an engagement ring after having only known me three weeks, our parents will have us committed."

He grinned, reluctantly letting go of her as she stood up and reclaimed her seat. He watched her as she picked up her knife and fork again, watching the dog as he begged for whatever she was eating. God, he was going to miss this. Just when he finally had what he wanted, he was going to have to leave it.

But in her statement about the weekend, he saw an opening to tell her what was on his mind. It was either that or he'd be leaving before she woke up, writing her a note like a coward.

"No, no rush," he agreed. "But I won't be around this weekend. In fact, I need to talk to you about it."

Kiki didn't sense any impending doom in his tone. She took a bite of chicken. "Oh?" she said. "Where are you going?"

Trace turned back to his food, hoping that he could ease her mind on this critical conversation if he acted casual about it. As if it wasn't breaking his heart to tell her what he was about to. He cut into his waffles.

"Let me back up a bit and preface this conversation," he said. "Let me tell you first that you can't repeat any of this. What I'm going to tell you can't leave this room. Okay?"

Kiki was serious but still not afraid or worried about what he was about to say. She nodded sincerely. "Of course," she said. "But why?"

He put a piece of waffle in his mouth. "You already know that I worked for the CIA for many years."

"Yes."

"That's actually why my friend Harry is here," he said. "To talk about something that I had to deal with a few years ago that's come back up again. I didn't finish it the first time and now I'm going to have to."

Kiki took another bite of chicken, listening with interest. "What is it?"

He swallowed the bite in his mouth, struggling to stay on an even keel so he wouldn't upset her. "I started out at the CIA as an analyst before moving into field operations," he said. "I can tell you that I was involved in espionage. I can also tell you that I have had to do some pretty James Bond-type stuff in my career. I became very good at what I did, so much so that I earned a nickname with allies and enemies alike. The Russians called me *istreblyat*."

Her brow furrowed. "Really?" she said, fascinated. "What does that mean?"

"Loosely translated, it means eliminator."

She cocked her head curiously. "Eliminator?" she said. She still wasn't really following him. "Why did they call you that?"

He sighed faintly and set his fork down. "Because if there was a dirty job to do, I was the one to do it," he said, seeing that she still wasn't really getting it. "If someone needed to be eliminated, I would do it."

Now, Kiki understood his meaning and her eyes widened. "Elimin –?" she couldn't even finish the word. "You...you would get rid of them?"

He nodded. "Any way I had to."

Her jaw dropped. "No," she hissed. "I don't believe it!"

"It's true."

"You were some kind of...of *assassin*?"

"Yes."

"Seriously?"

He nodded. "Seriously," he said. "Baby, you have to understand that I wasn't going to tell you any of this for a long time, if ever. I didn't want my past to enter our world. It's such a beautiful and peaceful world, and I've spent the past twenty years living in a hell of my own doing. I never knew life could be so wonderful until I met you and I don't want anything to ruin that. Does that make any sense?"

She was still looking at him through horrified eyes. "It does," she said, her voice oddly small. "But...a killer? Really, Trace?"

He could see her disbelief and he sighed again. "I did what I had to do for my country," he said. "It was my job. It wasn't anything I took any pleasure in. It was simply something that needed to be done and I was paid to do it. Please tell me I didn't make a mistake by telling you this."

Kiki shook her head quickly. "No, you didn't," she said. "But...I'm just having a tough time believing it, that's all. You are the sweetest, most normal man I've ever met and now you're telling me you had this secret life of being an... an assassin?"

"That's about the gist of it."

She set down her knife and fork completely, pushing her plate away. She wasn't hungry any longer. "Oh, my God," she breathed, struggling to come to grips with what he was telling her. "Jesse tried to tell me once that he thought you did more for the CIA, but I didn't believe him. You're saying that he was right?"

Trace frowned, deeply unhappy. "Did he really tell you that?"

"Did he really *know*?"

Trace shook his head. "No, he didn't know," he said, annoyed. "I never told him a thing, but he's always had a big imagination. I can't believe he said that to you."

Kiki could see that he was genuinely upset by it. "It was just in conversation," she said. "He wasn't trying to convince me of anything. He was just talking about his suspicions. I didn't believe him but it looks like I should have."

Trace shook his head. "That kind of thing needs to come from me. He didn't have any right to do that."

She reached out and touched his arm. "Don't be mad at him," she said. "He wasn't trying to be malicious about it. So what about this weekend? Where are you going? What's happening?"

He latched on to her hand, holding it tightly. Dinner, for the moment, was forgotten as they begin to delve into the heat of the conversation.

"A few years ago, I was assigned with taking out a Ukrainian mobster," he said. "The guy ran the Ukraine's biggest cartel—human trafficking, drugs, guns, you name it. Huge. Anyway, in the process of trying to eliminate the guy, one of my best friends was killed. After that, I walked away from my job and never looked back. I came out to California to start a new life away from that stuff. After Marcos died, I just couldn't do it anymore."

Now, his move to the West Coast was starting to make some sense. She'd remembered him speaking of it, back when they first became acquainted, and it had seemed like a difficult subject for him.

"You said you moved here because of your divorce," she said. "But it was more than that."

He nodded, caressing her hand. "Much more," he said.

"My wife and I were over for the most part, anyway. We had been for years. The divorce just made it official. Coming home to work for my dad last year was my way of trying to start fresh and forget about everything. So I assimilated myself into Rocklin Construction and then I met you three weeks ago. Honestly, baby, you couldn't have been more unexpected. Never in my life did I imagine to meet anyone like you."

She squeezed his fingers and he lifted her hand, kissing it. "You were pretty unexpected to me, too."

He grinned. "The best unexpected event I could have ever had," he said. Then, he sobered. "But back to your question about what is happening this weekend—I'm afraid I'm going to be gone longer than just the weekend."

She didn't like the sound of that. "How long, then?"

He shook his head, kissing her hand again. "I have no way of knowing," he said quietly. "I have a job to do and there's no knowing how long it will take."

She watched him as he rubbed her hand against his cheek. It was such a loving, longing gesture, one that pulled at her heart. She was beginning to feel very anxious. "You said you didn't finish a job," she said. "That's where you're going? To finish it?"

"Yes," he said. "For your own safety, you need to know what it is. Do you remember that guy who broke into your house a couple of weeks ago?"

She shuddered at the mere thought. "Yes, of course."

"I don't think he was random. I think he was here with a purpose."

She turned ashen. "What purpose?"

"I think he was looking for me," he said quietly. "Or, at the very least, he was going to try to get information from you as to my whereabouts. I'm not certain about that, but it's a possibility."

She was looking at him with her mouth hanging open. "*That's* why you wanted to move in so soon and protect me!"

"Yes," he said honestly. "It was possible that someone was after me and I was afraid they were going to try to get to you again."

Kiki stared at him. Then, she suddenly yanked her hand away from him, standing up from the dinner table. Both hands were over her mouth, a gesture of utter shock and dismay. Trace stood up, greatly distressed to see the expression on her face.

"You should have told me," she said as the tears began to come. "You should have told me what was going on, Trace. It wasn't fair not to tell me. And my girls...my God, my girls were here right after that happened. They could have been in danger, too!"

He moved to her quickly, wanting very badly to soothe her. "I'm sorry," he said steadily. "I'm still not sure that was what really happened and I didn't want to scare you. You'd only known me for two days, Kiki. You would think I was a lunatic if I told you my suspicions. In any case, the house is secure, the perimeter of the house is secure, and nothing else will happen, but just in case, I'm going to have Jesse come and stay with you while I'm gone. He'll be able to protect you if something...well, if something else happens."

Kiki dissolved in a flood of tears. "My God," she hissed. "What have you done, Trace? What kind of danger have you put me and my children in? You weren't honest about any of this, not in the least."

He was starting to lose his composure, terrified that his dreams and hopes for a future with her were about to come crashing down. "There was no point in telling you anything," he said, trying to be firm but gentle. "But I will admit that I was selfish. I have found the woman of my dreams and I don't want anything to ruin that. I'm sorry that I didn't tell you everything right from the start, but would it have mattered? Would it have made a difference in how you felt about me?"

Kiki was sobbing at this point. "It wasn't fair," she wept. "You let me fall in love with you and then you lowered the boom. Assassins chasing you? *Really?*"

He hung his head. "It's not like that, but..."

She cut him off. "You've put me at risk and my children at risk all because you didn't want anything to ruin our relationship," she said. "You know what? *You* ruined it with your dishonesty. There are men out to kill you and you couldn't even tell me that!"

He was beginning to panic. "I love you," he said. It was all he could think to say at the moment. "I love you so much, Kiki. I would never let anyone or anything hurt you. But the reality is that I didn't have a normal job for the past twenty years. Does that make me a monster? Of course it doesn't. What I did was in the line of duty for my country. I need you to understand that."

She just turned away from him, devastated. But she wasn't half as devastated as Trace was. He could feel something slipping away and he was unwilling to let it go. More than anything else in his entire life, he was going to fight for this until the bitter end.

She had to understand his position.

"I have to go to the Ukraine and eliminate the daughter of a man I was ordered to assassinate," he said, total truth on the table now. He wasn't going to hold anything back. "She is now head of her father's cartel and she wants to see me dead. There are a lot of people around her who would like to see her dead, too, so once she is gone, I believe that my problems will be over. I strongly believe that I have to do this in order to make sure you and I have a peaceful life. I want to open this bed and breakfast with you and be by your side, for better or for worse, 'til death do us part, but for that to happen, I have to pull one more job. It's just the way it is. I'm sorry if that is upsetting to you, baby, but I don't have a choice. I have to keep me safe and I have to keep you safe."

Kiki was slumped against the wall at this point, crying her heart out. She was horrified and terrified, for her and for her children and for Trace. All of the information had overwhelmed her and all she could think of was her fear and the fact that she felt Trace hadn't been forthright with her about any of this.

"You should have told me all of this at the first," she

said. "Maybe it would have been overwhelming to me, and scary, but at least you would have been up front and honest about it. Now, I feel as if I've been betrayed. You let me fall in love with someone who didn't exist. I fell in love with a normal guy who worked at a construction company and now I find out you're some kind of James Bond with people who are still trying to kill you. They almost killed me to get to you. And I have to deal with this for the rest of my life? You should have told me that from the start."

He sighed heavily, very much wanting to take her in his arms but knowing this wasn't the right moment. It would work badly for him if he tried.

"I'm sorry you feel that way," he said hoarsely. "It was never my intention to lie to you. My past was my past as far as I was concerned and I didn't see any reason to tell you about it. As far as people coming after me and trying to kill me, I have done my best to cover my tracks and slide into anonymity, but no system is perfect. Things could still happen and if they do, I will deal with them. But know that I will protect you with my life. You and your girls and that damn farting dog. You all mean the world to me and I would do anything for you. Please, Kiki...all I want is a normal life with you. I'm sorry if you feel betrayed but please know that was never my intention."

Kiki heard him but she was simply overcome with everything. She loved him; that was certain. Her guard was down, her emotions vulnerable, and she was deeply hurt and confused by what he had told her. She had no control left, her composure shattered. There was so much she wanted to say but she was afraid to, afraid she would say something she would regret. All she seemed to want to do was scream at him. Pushing herself off of the wall, she ran around him, giving him a wide berth, and raced up the back steps.

Trace followed her but he didn't get very far. She ran into her bedroom, slammed the door, and locked it. He stood at the door, heartbroken, listening to her weep. He even heard her vomit, several times, emptying her stomach of that beautiful meal she had so proudly made for him. Forehead against the old door, he called out to her softly.

"Kiki, I'm sorry, baby," he said. "I love you. I'll...I'll be right here in the hall if you need to talk. I'm not going anywhere."

She didn't answer. He didn't really expect her to. Shattered, he slumped against the door and sank down to his bottom, sitting there, listening to her hysteria on the other side. Not that he blamed her. It was true that he hadn't been totally forthcoming with her and that was on him. It was his fault. But he hoped that she would find it in her heart to forgive him.

He prayed she would.

As he sat there, he caught movement out of the corner of his eye to see that Stanley had pulled himself up the stairs and was now waddling over to him. Trace watched as the dog plopped down next to him, laying down, and he put a big hand on the pooch. With the other hand, he pulled his phone out of his pocket and texted Harry not to come. He'd meet him at the airport tomorrow. Putting his phone back into his pocket, he looked at the dog.

"Looks like it's just you and me tonight, Bullfrog," he said quietly.

The dog twitched in response.

In the dark upper hallway of Kiki's beastly house, Trace and Stanley stayed right outside of her bedroom all night.

FOURTEEN
TWO MONTHS LATER

HARRY KEPT LOOKING AT TRACE, sitting next to him in the upper-class section of the commercial aircraft as the jet gained altitude. It was evening so the cabin lights were dimmed, which was a good thing because Trace looked like he'd been through the meat grinder. He would have freaked everyone out in first class with his disheveled appearance.

The man had barely made the flight, a red-eye from Budapest to Washington. Harry had been waiting for Trace at Ferenc Liszt International Airport in Budapest for six hours, praying the man would make it. He'd been in communication with Trace daily for the past eight weeks, using their ground contacts to follow and finally locate Nathalia Nevredevova and her henchmen. Two days ago Trace had informed him that he was about to make his move. The rendezvous at Budapest's airport had been set.

All Trace had to do was finish his duty and make that plane.

Damn, he'd cut it close.

It had been one of the few glitches in a mission that had otherwise gone smoothly. It had actually been fairly easy to locate Nathalia because she was arrogant like her father and traveled in the open for the most part with an armed escort that would have put the American president's detail to shame. She also liked to spend money and would haunt high-end shops to spend her father's millions on purses and furs and shoes.

Therefore, it really hadn't been difficult to find the woman. Trace, being familiar with her locale, her friends, and her usual places, simply went back to the area he knew she was operating in. Her family practically owned the city of Zhytomyr and that was where he started. With a three-man cell shadowing his every move and feeding him intel, Trace went back into the thick of it to remove Nathalia from power. He kept his eye on the prize, on the hope for a peaceful life for him and Kiki when all was said and done, and that's the beacon of light that kept him going.

He needed that beacon considering how he and Kiki had parted. Every day, thoughts of her filled his heart and mind and every day, he was torn apart by his own sense of selfishness and dishonesty when it came to her. She had been right, about everything, and he wanted so badly to tell her that. He wasn't sure he'd ever get the opportunity but he'd made the decision early on that no matter what happened, he would return to her when he was finished with his mission. He would go back to that half-finished house and find closure, good or bad.

Even if she didn't want to see him again, she could at least tell him to his face. But that would have to come from her. Until she said it and he walked away, forever, he was going on the hope that whatever had happened between them was fixable. If he thought of it any other way, he couldn't go on.

And he had to go on.

So he pushed forward, entrenching himself in the Ukraine once again. It was so strange; even though he hadn't been there for a few years, it was as if he never left. The smells were still the same, the sights and sounds as he remembered them. Everything smelled like gasoline and cabbage. He couldn't describe it any other way.

All he knew was that he hated it.

But he plugged on, shadowing Nathalia and her men, showing up in outdoor cafes and nightclubs and shopping venues where she was. He was scouting out her security these days, wanting to get a handle on how easy it would be to abduct her. He found that she was the sloppiest in the nightclubs, where she would wander around while her detail stayed to the tables. That was the Nathalia he knew; she wanted to be seen as single and sexy and she couldn't do that with a bunch of goons hanging around her.

Finally, eight weeks after arriving in the Ukraine, Trace had his chance to get to her. He had planned his moves, his escape, and nothing was going to stop him. If anything did, it would be those goons with the Glock 9mm guns concealed beneath their sport coats. But he wasn't going to make an easy target for them.

The Eliminator was back and he was meaner than ever.

It was a nightclub called the Crystal Sky and he'd come in through the kitchens, mingling with the workers and finally the patrons to lose himself in the crowd. Nathalia was there that night with girlfriends, which was unusual for her. She usually didn't like the competition. Trace paid a handsome young man in a crisp silk suit to ask her to dance and take her into a private room. When the young man brought her into the room with promises of dancing and even sex, Trace was waiting for her.

Like the spider to the fly, he had her.

The young man, very well paid, quickly left the room as Trace swooped in on Nathalia, who tried to scream but he managed to render her unconscious before dragging her out through the back of the club. Meanwhile, the young man left the club without Nathalia's goons being wise to what had happened. They thought she was in the back having sex with the guy and waited at least two hours before going to look for her. By that time, it was too late. Trace had her out of the city.

And that was the last anyone ever saw of Nathalia Nevredevova.

It was an odd event for Trace, really. Hands that had touched Kiki so tenderly were capable of killing. It was his job, his duty, but the fact remained that he was fully capable of such things. It was a strange dilemma, to be sure, but he tried not to think about it. After the task was completed, Trace had stolen a car and made a mad dash for the border of Hungary and then on to Budapest where his flight back to the States waited.

He didn't think he'd been followed, but he kept changing highways, taking smaller roads, all of it designed to throw off any tails that might be on to him. He'd just taken out the head of the Nevredev Cartel. It wasn't until he'd entered Hungary on his American passport that he'd heard, in a restaurant when he'd stopped to grab some food, that the Nevredev Cartel had fractured in the wake of Nathalia's death. Fractured and destroyed, or at least that was what the news anchor had said. And with that news, Trace breathed a sigh of relief.

He'd accomplished what he'd set out to do.

Now, he found himself on a plane next to Harry as the aircraft ascended to cruising altitude. Neither man had said a word, at least not yet. Trace kept his focus on the view from the window as the plane soared into the night sky. It wasn't until they were nearly a full hour into their flight that Harry finally spoke.

"Are you okay, Trace?" he asked quietly.

Trace nodded. "Fine."

"Is there anything you need?"

"No."

Harry didn't say anything more. He glanced across the aisle where the two other intel men sat, lifting his eyebrows at them as if to suggest that Trace wasn't fine at all. But no one pushed the man. The Eliminator had been in action one last time and the results were impressive. It was his prerogative if he wanted to talk about it or not.

Chances were that he wouldn't until he was forced to.

A flight attendant came around with glasses of champagne for the upper-class passengers and Harry took two, silently handing one over to Trace. Trace took the glass, downed it in one swallow, and then took Harry's glass and downed that one, too. It was then, and only then, did he speak.

"I saw the news when I crossed the border into Hungary," he said. "Is it true?"

Harry knew what he meant. "It's true," he said. "Nevredev is so fractured they'll never recover. No one gives a damn about Nathalia and her petty crap, and especially about her sense of vengeance when it came to you. It's over, man. You did it."

Trace took a deep breath, pondering that information. The flight attendant came back with more champagne and he took two more flutes, downing them like shots of tequila. Harry quietly asked the flight attendant to bring them a bottle. When the man left to go up front for the alcohol, Harry turned to Trace.

"Ease up, Trace," he said quietly. "It's over. You did your job and it's over."

Trace was feeling the alcohol in his veins a bit. "You're damn right it's over," he said. "I've done my bit for king and country and you're going to leave me the hell alone from now on. I'm going back to California and back to Kiki, if she'll have me. I don't want to see your ugly face again."

Harry sighed faintly. "I thought you said she wasn't speaking to you."

Trace grunted, unhappy and weary. "I don't know what she's doing," he said. "All I know is that I'm going to go back to her and try to make things right between us. I should have told her everything from the start, Harry. It wasn't that she was upset about my job or my past. It was the fact that I kept it from her and didn't let her in on what I thought about the break-in at her house and the fact that Ukrainian operatives might be after me. It was the omission of the truth she was upset with and she had ever right."

Harry had heard this before, the night they had departed Los Angeles International Airport for Dulles in Washington. He looked at Trace, dirty and beaten and bloodied, smelling like he hadn't had a shower in a week.

"If she doesn't take you back, I will," he said. "You're the best of the best, Trace. The past eight weeks were like old times again, when you and Marcos and Beau and Reed were an unbeatable team. You know we need men like you and for you to walk away...well, I've said it before. It's a waste of material."

Trace scratched his head, exhausted and agitated. "Maybe," he said. "But I can't do this anymore. It took everything I had to come here and do this job and now that it's over, I have nothing left. I don't want to be operating alone for the rest of my life, Harry. I want a partner in life and that's Kiki. I want a nice, normal job and her to come home to every night. It's the fairytale I want."

"Is that all it is? A fairytale?"

Trace shook his head. "I didn't mean it like that," he said. "I just meant that every time I look at her, or touch her, it feels like a fairytale. It feels like everything I've ever dreamt of and I'm not about to let that go. I'll beg, plead, and cry any way I have to in order to have her forgiveness."

Harry simply nodded. "Then I wish you luck, I really do," he said. "But before you do that, you have a debriefing when you arrive in Washington. The State Department and our department heads are going to want your entire report. When that's done, you can go back to California."

Trace knew the routine. He'd been through it enough times before. He leaned his head against the back of the seat, relaxing for the first time in weeks. He'd slept little and ate even less during his hunt for Nathalia and now it was just starting to dawn on him that he could finally relax. He could finally breathe.

This time, it was really over for good.

"I didn't mean what I said, Harry."

"About what?"

"About not seeing your ugly face again. You're welcome to come to California any time."

Harry smiled ironically. "Your lady friend may not want to see me," he said. "She may have a bigger grudge against me than she has against you for pulling you back into this."

Trace shook his head. "She won't have a grudge," he said. "She's got a remarkable capacity for forgiveness and I can't believe that would end with me. Did I ever tell you about her husband dying about a year ago?"

Harry shook his head. "You haven't told me much about her at all."

Trace's entire body began to relax even more, especially now with thoughts of Kiki on his mind. He turned his head, looking out of the window into the brilliant night sky.

"Her husband died suddenly last year of a heart attack," he murmured, thoughts of Kiki heavy on his brain now. "At the funeral, some guy showed up and to make a long story short, this guy turned out to be her husband's gay lover. But you know what? She forgave him. I wouldn't have been so magnanimous but she found it in her heart to forgive the man. I just can't believe that she can't forgive me, too. She's too compassionate and reasonable a woman not to. But I'm not going to assume anything. And I'm not going to give up, not ever."

Harry listened to him ramble, rather sleepily now. The four shots of champagne were taking effect. He felt rather sorry for a man as torn up as Trace was. Love and duty and forgetting one's past sometimes didn't mix but he hoped for Trace's sake that it would work out. The man deserved a little happiness for once and that fairytale that people only dreamed about.

"Well, I'm sure it will all work out in the end," he said. "Meanwhile, get some sleep. You've earned it."

The words weren't even out of his mouth before he heard Trace snoring.

FIFTEEN

THE HOUSE WAS silent and still at dusk. The Santa Ana winds had picked up again, clearing the sky and giving way to a spectacular sunset.

Inside the old kitchen with its old linoleum floor, Kiki was making a light supper for herself. She hadn't eaten much in the past several weeks, ever since that disastrous dinner of chicken and waffles that she'd made for Trace. She just couldn't face cooking anything with enthusiasm anymore, ever since that night when his past had come to light and she hadn't been able to handle it.

God, it seemed so long ago. Like a lifetime ago. That night, she'd retreated to her room and hadn't come out until noon the next day, when she heard his truck fire up and leave the driveway. It was so strange - she was so confused about everything and as long as she knew he was outside of her door, she couldn't face him. She was angry with him, and terrified for him, and terrified for her and her children. He'd frightened her so much with what he'd told her and all of the begging in the world, the pleading for her to be understanding, couldn't ease that fear. It was something she'd had to settle in her own mind.

It was something she needed to do without looking into his anxious face. She just didn't want to look at him, knowing he'd selfishly put her in harm's way. But the moment his truck left the driveway, she'd come out of her room and went downstairs to find Stanley snoring on his bed in the kitchen with a rolled-up piece of paper stuck into his collar. It had been enough to soften her as she'd pulled the note out and read it.

Words can't express how much I love you. I'm sorry if you feel betrayed. I'm sorry if I hurt you. Please know I wouldn't have knowingly done that for the world. But if you don't want me to come back, I understand. I just want you to be happy.
All my love,
Trace

The gentle note had dissolved her into tears, once more, and she'd sobbed off and on the rest of the day. She was coming to understand why he'd done what he'd done, struggling to look at it from his perspective, but she was having difficulty reconciling the fact that the man hadn't been open with her. That was her big hang-up. At least if he had been honest, especially after the break-in, she would have had time to reconcile herself to the way things were going to be. But he hadn't. He'd kept it from her and she had fallen hard for what she had believed to be a nice, normal guy. But he hadn't been normal in the least.

He was a killer.

Truthfully, that part didn't really bother her. He was a spy, a patriot, and that wasn't an issue. In fact, she was rather proud that he was so dedicated to his country. But the lack of openness...she was coming to think that maybe he just didn't know how to be open. Being a CIA operative, it wasn't like he could talk about his job. Maybe he'd just gotten used to concealing everything, even from someone he loved. He'd dug himself into a hole with Kiki and by the time he'd been forced to tell her the truth, she felt blindsided, like their entire relationship had been a lie.

But it wasn't a lie.

Kiki loved him and that was the truth. He was kind and generous and humorous, and they laughed a lot and enjoyed many of the same things. He loved her girls and he loved her stinky dog. He was great at conversation, intelligent to a fault, and she loved the way he looked at her. Such a sexy, smoldering look that set her on fire. By five o'clock on the day he'd left, her resistance was coming down and she called his cell phone but was met with a message that it was no longer in service. Sick and depressed, all she could do was pick up the pieces of her life, the new life she'd wanted to start for herself in Pasadena, and move on.

Now, all of these weeks later, that's where she found herself but with some changes. She stopped all work on the house even though she had a contract with Rocklin. She'd called Shaun two days after Trace had left and told him that she was putting the restoration on hold indefinitely. She gave him a lot of financial reasons and he gallantly told her he'd hold the price for the next few months, but the truth was that she really didn't know what she wanted to do.

Rocklin Construction reminded her of Trace and she just couldn't face seeing their trucks every day, slapping her in the face with what she'd lost. Rick Rocklin had even come to see her but she hadn't answered the door. She watched him come and go from a window, hidden from view. She didn't want to talk to him, either. It seemed that all of her dreams left with Trace and she didn't want to face those memories anymore.

Now, she just wanted out.

There was a *For Sale* sign in front of the house now and she'd had a lot of activity on it. It had been listed for eight days and she'd had a dozen people come through it with three possible offers. She was asking a lot, more than she'd bought it for, but people seemed willing to pay it with the finished floors, partially finished walls, completed electrical and plumbing.

After selling the house, her big plans consisted of moving in with her parents until she could figure out what she wanted to do. She was defeated and crushed, and that lovely future she'd hoped for with Trace was gone. It was all she could do now to get out of bed every morning.

So the light supper she'd made herself on this evening

was the first meal she'd had all day. Stanley sat next to her chair, hoping for a piece of chicken from her salad, and she fed the dog a couple of pieces while she absently watched the evening news. She told her mom she'd come over later but she wasn't feeling much like visiting with her parents, who were genuinely concerned for her. All of the chaos in losing Mark, and now in losing the love of her life in Trace, was proving to be a lot for Kiki to take. The normally strong woman was showing signs of cracking.

As she picked at the salad, she noticed a headline on the news that said something about the Ukraine with a byline of an assassination. Anything about the Ukraine over the past six weeks had Kiki's interest and she turned up the volume.

"...sources say that she inherited the position from her father, Osto Nevredev, and the Nevredev Cartel was one of the most powerful in the Ukraine. But that all came to a halt several days ago when her body was found in a burned-out car on the outskirts of Kiev near the cemetery where her father was buried. U.S. intelligence officials have hailed her death as a blow against the Nevredev organized crime syndicate, as it seems to be crumbling already with several different factions now vying for control of the Nevredev territory. The U.S. considers this latest development a victory in the war against foreign organized crime. In other news, the stock market has...."

Kiki shut off the television. She sat there for a moment, shocked to the bone at what she'd just heard, but there was no doubt in her mind that Trace had been at the heart of the event. It was everything he'd told her he needed to do and it was evident that he'd carried out his job. *I have to go to the Ukraine and eliminate the daughter of a man I was ordered to assassinate.*

Dear God...it looked like he had, after all.

The news had her reeling. Now, Trace was all she could think of. She'd done a pretty good job of erasing him from her mind over the past few weeks but now he was back, full-force, and he occupied every waking moment.

Had he survived? Was he okay? Was he coming home now or had he decided to go back to the CIA? So many questions in her mind. No longer hungry, Kiki stood up from the table and dumped her salad into the trash, feeding a few more pieces of chicken to Stanley as he danced around beside her. The dog grew fat on the food she couldn't eat as she grew progressively thinner. Her clothes were hanging on her now but she didn't much care. In truth, she didn't much care about anything these days.

Except Trace.

Washing her plate, she thought of the last time she saw Trace in this kitchen, as he tried to tell her of his Ukrainian mission, and her heart hurt for him. Everything hurt for him. She'd never missed someone so much in her entire life, wondering for the hundredth time if she'd overreacted when he told her his dark secrets. She still didn't think she had, but that was all water under the bridge now. Trace was gone, for good, and there was no way for her to contact him to tell him she was sorry for reacting so poorly to his news, not even through his family. She didn't want to drag them into the drama. She still loved Trace and always would, but the damage to their relationship had been done.

It was over.

Drying the dish and putting it back in the cabinet, her cell phone rang and she looked at the caller I.D. to see that it was Embry. Distracted from thoughts of dead female mobsters and Trace Rocklin, she answered.

"Hello?"

Embry's voice was loud and cheery on the other side. "Hi, Mom!" she said. "Es and I are coming up for the weekend, okay?"

Kiki smiled faintly at the sound of her daughter's voice. "Sure," she said. "Come on up. I...I haven't seen you two in a while. Lots to talk about."

There was music and giggling in the background. "I know," Embry said. "We've just been really busy at school. Sorry we haven't been up in a while. How is the house coming along?"

The question brought tears to Kiki's eyes. She hadn't seen her daughters since they'd met Trace and she had purposely not told them of the drama going on because she really didn't think they needed to know. She wasn't one to cry all over someone's shoulder about her problems and she definitely didn't want to pull her daughters into her relationship drama, so they didn't know a thing. They didn't even know that she was selling the house. She tried not to cry as she spoke.

"It's still here," she said. "The floors have been refinished. They're really gorgeous. It's a work in progress."

More music and laughter in the background. "We can't wait to see it," Embry said. "How's the boyfriend?"

Lots of laughter in the background with that question, coming from her two giddy girls, but Kiki nearly broke down. Tears rolled down her cheeks as she struggled not to sound like she was upset.

"Oh...wow," she said. "Lots to tell you about that, too."

"Really? What?"

"We'll talk about it when you get here."

A pause. "Mom, are you okay?"

"I'm fine. When will you be here?'

Embry groaned. "We're on the 5 Freeway heading north," she said. "We're only in Del Mar and it's a parking lot. We'll be lucky if we're there by midnight."

"Okay," Kiki said. "Drive carefully. I'll see you when you get here."

"Okay. Love you!"

"Love you both."

Kiki hung up the phone and set it on the counter, using a paper towel to wipe the tears from her eyes. They were always so close to the surface these days. Over near the back door, Stanley whined to be let out so she opened the door, watching the dog bolt. She thought he must have had to relive himself badly to move that fast, so she left the door open while she went in search of her shoes.

Kiki liked to walk the yard a lot, looking at the plants that were beginning to take shape, and inspecting the property that would soon belong to someone else. She'd whispered apologies to the house a thousand times about that -

apologizing that she was too weak to face the memory of Trace within the old walls. She hoped the house understood.

In shorty-shorts that were hanging on her slender frame and a tank top that showed a twenty-pound weight loss, she slipped her flip-flops on and went out the back door, following Stanley's trail. Instinctively, she peered around the backside of the house, over where the driveway was, half-expecting to see Jesse and his camper still parked out on the street.

Jesse had taken his request to watch over her very seriously but Kiki wouldn't let him in the house after she and Trace parted ways. Jesse told her that Trace had specifically called him from the airport on the day he left for Washington to make sure he kept an eye on her, but Kiki told him to go away and shut the door in his face.

Not to be deterred, Jesse literally camped out on the street every night in his pickup truck, now fitted with an overhead-cab camper on the back. It went on for at least a month until Pasadena Parking Enforcement laid two big tickets on him and then he'd had to go. By then, there was no more construction at the house, no more people, and Kiki clearly didn't want him there. Dejected, Jesse had given up his post but Kiki still half-expected to see him there.

She rather missed him, too.

It was warm on this mid-December day as she ambled around her yard, pulling at weeds and looking at the new growth that was trying to sprout. The fountain, that massive and impressive thing, was flowing away at full-steam and she spent a lot of time by it, finding peace in the lily pads and little fish that were now swimming about.

She glanced up every once in a while, seeing Stanley up by the front gate, nosing around in the bushes. He disappeared into a big nest of vines and bushes near the gate itself and she could hear him moving around in the bramble. As the dog nosed around, she turned back to the water, watching the fish and thinking how much she would miss the fountain when she left.

The fountain.

It was such a beautiful feature. It was the first place she'd ever laid eyes on Trace and every time she saw it, it reminded her of him. How many conversations had they had about the fountain as the center of their bed and breakfast/ wedding venue, where people could get married against it, soothed by the sounds of the waters from the *Agua de la Vida?* Trace had had some very big plans for the area surrounding the fountain—laying paver stones that would look like a vintage pathway and growing flowering vines behind it so it would make a beautiful backdrop in pictures. He'd had some great ideas for it but they were ideas that would never come to fruition now. At least they got the fountain running, though.

She swirled her hand in the waters of the fountain, watching the fish amongst the lily pads, hearing Stanley off behind her still rummaging through the leaves. She caught sight of some weeds over to her right, on the other side of the fountain, and she went over to them, kneeling down to pull them up. Even if she was leaving the house, still, the garden was special to her. The whole house was important to her. It was breaking her heart to sell it. Stanley was behind her by then, brushing up against her leg, and she happened to glance over at the dog.

And then, she saw it.

A piece of paper attached to Stanley's collar. It took her a moment to realize what she was seeing and, puzzled, she reached out to take it. Suddenly, she was seized with excitement and hope and...*oh, God, is it really a note in his collar?* She grabbed at it and pulled it away, only to realize that it was a scrap of trash that had gotten hooked into his collar. It was just part of a flyer that had somehow ended up on the bushes where nosy Stanley had picked it up. Tears of disappointment sprang to her eyes as she crumpled it up and angrily tossed it away.

"Hi."

A voice came from behind, a male voice, and Kiki was so startled that she ended up falling forward onto her knees. She knew that voice; God help her, she knew that voice and she bolted to her feet, turning around to see that Trace was standing several feet away, back over by the fountain. The sight of him startled her to the bone. Kiki had to slap her hands over her mouth to keep from crying out.

The paper in the collar...had it been a sign? She wondered wildly. *Had he put it there to break the news that he had come back?*

"Oh, my God," Trace said as he got a good look at her.

Tears came to his eyes as he simply stood there and gazed at her. "You've lost so much weight. Are you okay? Kiki, why is the house up for sale?"

She could hardly speak. "You...you're alive."

He could barely hear her. "Of course I am," he said gently. "Did you think I wouldn't be?"

"I...I didn't know."

He could see how stunned she was. He repeated his question. "Why is the house up for sale?"

Kiki was having difficulty processing his query, her brain overwhelmed by his unexpected appearance. "Because," she said. "I...I can't stay here."

"Why not?"

A sob bubbled out. "Because I have to go," she said. "It...this place...you're everywhere. It reminds me of you and I can't stay here and see you every hour of every day, in the walls and in the rooms and everything. You're everywhere."

His heart sank. "Oh...God," he breathed. "I'm so sorry, Kiki. I guess I shouldn't have come back but...but the way we left it...I didn't know *how* we left it and I just got back into town. If you don't want to see me again, I just need to know. I didn't want to assume anything."

Tears were brimming in her eyes and she closed them, spilling rivers of tears all over her cheeks and the hands that were still over her mouth. Everything in her was trying to break out into gut-busting sobs but she held fast.

Like a dream from another time, Trace was standing before her in all of his handsome glory. It was a moment she never truly thought would come and there were things she had to say to him. She had to get it out so he could hear it all, whether or not he wanted to.

"I'm sorry I got so mad at you," she said, her voice tight. "I'm so, so sorry I treated you like that. I had no right...I was scared and what you told me was so overwhelming and I just didn't handle it well. It was like a nightmare and I just...I just didn't handle it well at all. I'm so sorry."

He took a few steps toward her, blinking the tears in his eyes, splattering them. "No," he said hoarsely. "*I'm* sorry. I should have told you everything from the beginning but I didn't want to spoil the beauty of the world we were creating. I didn't want to mess anything up. Maybe it was my way of pretending nothing but you existed, or had ever existed. You were right when you said that I had put you at risk. I was arrogant to think that I was the only one it was affecting. That was wrong. Even if you don't want to see me again, to know that you forgive me...I would be grateful if you could."

He sounded so truly sad and repentant. Her heart, so confused and fragile as of late, still had the capacity for great forgiveness. The whole situation was her fault, his fault, and nobody's fault. It had just happened, a terribly string of reactions and overreactions that brought them to this place.

But she was the only one who could make it right and she knew it. He was here, begging for forgiveness. She did the only thing she could do.

"Of course I forgive you," she said. "I never thought I'd

have the chance to tell you that. The day you left, I tried to call you but your phone was out of service. I figured you just...well, that you just didn't want to talk to me anymore. After the way I screamed at you, I don't blame you. I thought you were gone forever."

He wiped the moisture off his face, a faint glow coming to his eyes. It was the glow of hope, that maybe whatever had happened between them really wasn't the end. It was that hope that had kept him going for the past eight weeks. Every time he felt like giving up, or every time he reached an obstacle that seemed insurmountable, that hope was there, the hope that Kiki would still be there at the end of the rainbow.

"No," he said softly. "Not gone forever, not at all. I'm not angry with you. I never was. I just want to make things right between us again, Kiki. Is that even possible?"

She pondered that a moment. "I think so," she said. "I hope so. Trace, I was selling the house because of it reminds me of you. It wasn't because I hated you or couldn't stand the thought of you. It was because of the pain I felt every time I remembered you standing in the kitchen or sitting on the porch. Your imprint is everywhere. I really didn't think you were coming back to me and I just couldn't stay here any longer."

He smiled faintly, a massive amount of relief in his expression. "You are the only thing that has kept me going," he said. "I love you more than I ever did, Kiki. I swear to you that there won't be any more withholdings or half-truths. It's just that I've operated that way for the past twenty years. I've had to in order to protect my identity. I did it with you and I shouldn't have. I swear to you I won't ever do that again."

Her pale lips twitched with a smile. "I believe you."

"Do you really?"

"I do."

"Can we fix this, then?"

It was the question she wanted to hear, the hope for a future she thought she'd lost. At that point, she couldn't even hold back; she ran at him and he opened his arms out to her. She remembered throwing herself into his embrace, but little else after that. It was as if she was in a fog, something that filled her and hazed her mind, but it was a fog of relief and passion and adoration like nothing she had ever experienced. All of it, the fog and the joy and the passion, was Trace.

He was back, and he was here to stay.

Kiki didn't even realize she'd run to him. Suddenly, she was in his arms, her mouth fusing to his, her arms around his neck and her legs around his waist. Trace kissed her furiously, forcefully enough to drive her teeth into her soft lip. It was power beyond passion, a moment in time that they didn't think they'd ever experience again.

It was pain draining away.

It was love returning.

Everything was going to be okay.

Somehow, they made it to the porch and into the house. Trace tore his mouth away from hers long enough to call the dog, who took his sweet time meandering back into the house. Trace kicked the door shut behind him, and managed to lock it, but his goal was clear. The same goal he'd had the night he left her, before the situation between them had grown so awful. He was going to *show* her how much he loved her.

Words were no longer necessary.

Taking the stairs, he kicked open the door to the bedroom he once rented. He didn't even notice that it hadn't been touched since he'd left. Kiki had made his bed the morning he'd gone to work and she hadn't touched it since. He lay her down on top of the comforter, kissing the flesh of her cleavage, feasting on her skin. Kiki closed her eyes to the ecstasy of it, feeling every kiss even as she unbuttoned her shorts and pulled her tank top over her head. Trace let go of her long enough to yank her shorts and underwear off, removing his own shirt.

There was that gorgeous chest that Kiki remembered.

Reaching up, she pulled him down to her, latching to his mouth even as he fumbled with his jeans. Once he managed to get them off, Trace lowered himself onto her, his hands in her hair, on her shoulders, stroking her belly before moving down her thighs. She was hot and delicious, her soft body pressed against him, and he eventually cupped her face as his lips ravaged hers, his tongue invading her mouth and tasting her sweetness. He'd never gotten any further than this with her before, but tonight that was going to change.

His hands moved lower.

Kiki groaned when a big hand closed over her left

breast and his mouth left hers to clamp down on a tender nipple. He suckled hard and she cried out softly, never more aroused in her entire life. Kiki wasn't shy about parting her legs for him and he stroked her thighs, experiencing their silken texture before his fingers moved to the fluff of curls between her legs only to discover she was slick and wet. She was ready for him. His mouth on hers, he plunged his fingers into her quivering body and she gasped, lifting her pelvis to meet his hand.

Trace didn't make her wait.

He mounted her and thrust deep as her hot, wet body closed in around him. It was the most amazing thing he had ever experienced and as he thrust into her, listening to her grunts of pleasure, he let his body do the talking. Telling her how much he loved her. He'd never known anything like it in his life, an uncontrollable attraction to a woman he couldn't live without. A woman he couldn't breathe without. It was a moment he'd waited for his entire life, a moment he wasn't even sure would ever come.

But here it was.

And it was more than he had dreamed of.

Kiki's orgasm came with swift pants and a stiffening body, and he fingered a taut nipple, working her through the spasms, prolonging her pleasure as he suckled her breasts. As she struggled to catch her breath, another one washed over her and Trace moved his hands down to her buttocks, holding her pelvis against his as he thrust hard and deep. She met his thrusts, grinding her hips against him, until he felt her release yet again. Unable to hold it back any longer, Trace climaxed hard.

He was fairly certain he'd blacked out.

But, somehow, he came around. He was laying on her, holding her tightly, thinking about the fact that for whatever stupid reasons he'd waited to go to bed with her, he was kind of glad they *had* waited. It made the moment so much more amazing. Her soft body against his was like something out of a romance novel, like they were made for one another.

Two pieces of the same puzzle.

Eventually, he shifted so his body weight wasn't on top of her as their passion cooled, but he made no attempt to move off of her or even withdraw. He just lay there and held her. Gently, he kissed her head, her cheek, her neck. Each kiss was a silent declaration of love, each touch was a silent chorus of adoration. He touched, he stroked, and in a short amount of time, he grew hard again and began to thrust into her, slowly but powerfully. Kiki held fast to him, letting the man do what he wanted to do, relishing the feel of him.

However he wanted to do it was fine with her.

Trace wanted to do it on her, behind her, with her on him, and finally with her under him once again. They made love, they kissed, and each touch healed the pain of separation and longing they'd suffered through. Each kiss, each touch, healed so much in both of them.

It was cathartic on many levels.

Near midnight, they finally lay in each other's arms,

wrapped up in Trace's comforter. Kiki dozed off, but he wasn't asleep. He never felt less like sleeping in his life. He wanted to savor every second, every breath, and every touch.

This was what life was about.

Thank God he'd been given a second chance with her.

"Are you asleep?" Kiki asked softly.

He kissed her on the forehead. "No," he said. "I thought you were."

She yawned. "Not really," she said. "What are you thinking about?"

"That I love you."

She lifted her head to look at him. "And I love you," she murmured, leaning in to kiss him gently. "That has never changed."

He smiled faintly, tucking a stray piece of hair behind her ear. "I'm overwhelmed by everything," he said. "But that's a good thing. I feel like the luckiest man alive."

She smiled faintly, watching his expression in the dim light. "What happens now?"

"What do you mean?"

She lay back down against him. "I mean you've come back," she said. "Are you going back to work for your dad?"

"Yes," he said. "Eventually. I was thinking about taking a few weeks off and just hanging around the house with you. Maybe helping the construction guys work on it."

"I stopped the work on it, Trace," she said. The mood threatened to dampen. "Thinking you weren't coming back...and I was selling it...I just couldn't bear doing any more work on it. I don't mean to bring it all up again, but maybe we should talk about it just to get it out in the open and make sure it doesn't rise again. The past eight weeks have been one of the worst times of my life and I don't want it coming back again and again."

He gave her a gentle squeeze. "I understand that," he said. "I think it would be healthy for us to talk about it and get it all out so there are no questions, no misunderstandings. But do you really want to do it now?"

"No," she said. Then, she snorted. "Not now. But tomorrow. Or the next day, maybe. But not now. This moment...this is our moment. I'm not ready to give it up just yet."

He laughed softly. "Me, either."

Trace was about to go in for another deep kiss when they suddenly heard a door slam. His head shot up, along with Kiki's, as Stanley, who was in the hall outside the bedroom door, began to bark. Trace was halfway out of bed when they began to hear voices downstairs.

"It's the girls," Kiki said, leaping out of bed. "I completely forgot they were on their way home for the weekend."

Trace began to laugh. "Jesus," he said. "And they catch us in bed together? We're doing just what we told them we weren't going to do!"

Kiki hissed at him. "Shush!" she said, but she was starting to laugh because he was. "Get in bed and stay there. Don't come out."

"Why not?"

"If you're my tenant, you're supposed to be asleep," she said, waving frantically at him. "Go to bed!"

Grabbing her clothes, she slinked across the dark hallway but not before shutting his bedroom door. As Trace sat there, the comforter across his lap, he could hear the girls coming up the stairs whispering loudly.

"Mom?" Embry said, knocking softly on Kiki's bedroom door. "Mom, are you awake?"

He could hear Kiki answering, muffled, and she made a good show of sounding like she had been asleep. The girls went into her bedroom, talking to her, and Trace reasoned that no normal human being could sleep through their chatter, so he got up and put on pajama bottoms and a t-shirt. Feigning a yawn, he opened the door and wanted to know about the party going on in Kiki's room. Embry and Esme were delighted to see him and, truthfully, he was delighted to see them, too. They both rushed at him to give him a big hug.

It was the best greeting he could have possibly imagined.

From the old cities of the Ukraine to the halls of Washington, DC, to the mountains of Pasadena, Trace's life had come full circle. As he'd told Harry, he'd done his bit for king and country, and now he was living for himself.

Him and Kiki, those giggly girls, and that farting dog.

Finally, Trace Rocklin had come home.

EPILOGUE
TWO MONTHS LATER

THE WEDDING FOUNTAIN finally lived up to its name when Kiki and Trace were married standing in front of it on a bright February day, the spectacular antique fountain that had spilled out the waters of life for well over one hundred years. Now, the fountain itself was living again, a symbol of all things that continued on. The symbol of those starting a new life together.

With only close family as witnesses–Bill and Sylvia Wickham, Jim Wickham, Jesse and Shaun and Rick Rocklin, Trace's son, Alex, and the still-giggling Esme and Embry Conrad, Kiki and Trace said their vows to the gentle sounds of the fountain that had come to mean so much to them. It was where they first met and now where they swore to be true to each other for the rest of their lives. They promised to love, honor, and cherish one other until the end of time as Stanley milled around their feet, participating as best a dog could.

When the wedding officiant gave his final blessing, Trace kissed his new wife for the first time as Jesse and Shaun whistled and hooted, causing Trace and Kiki to break down into laughter. But it didn't matter; everything about this day was full of joy and laughter, and a new life for two people who had been so very lost before finding one another. A new day, and a new chapter, had finally begun for Trace and Kiki Rocklin.

Later that night, after the guests had left and Embry, Esme, and Alex were up in the finished attic coming to know each other now that they were siblings, Kiki and Trace sat out on the dark front porch, watching the fountain in the moonlight, pondering the very busy day and watching Stanley mill around in the darkness.

Kiki sat on Trace's lap as he gently rocked her back and forth on the new patio rocker. In fact, nearly everything was new now at *Agua de la Vida* and they'd already had several bed and breakfast guests as well as having had two micro-weddings. The kitchen, the last thing to be remodeled, was nearly finished and the rest of the house shined like a new penny. It was a time of change and excitement as Austin Glen's old house began to live a new life as well.

"What's on the agenda for tomorrow?" Trace asked his wife. "Alex has got to fly back to Chicago in a couple of days so I was thinking we should take the kids somewhere and bond as a family. I know our kids are adults, but they should still get to know each other."

Kiki nodded. "I haven't really thought about it but you're right," she said, watching Stanley sniff around the fountain. "I've been so consumed thinking about our wedding and the future weddings we have booked that I haven't thought about much else."

Trace grinned, giving her a hug. "Be careful what you wish for, right?" he said. "You wanted a successful bed and breakfast and micro-wedding venue. Looks like you've got it."

She grinned. "Seems like a dream," she said. "Life has a funny way of turning out sometimes."

"Any regrets?"

"God, no."

"Good," he said. "But we do need to get that kitchen finished. Maybe I'll have to tackle the last of it myself."

"Are you sure?" she said. "The kitchen contractor seems to be doing a good job."

"He is, but he's slow. We need to get it done."

"Do you have the time? Your dad is keeping you pretty busy."

He poo-pooed her. "Piece of cake," he said. "Besides, I'll get Jess to help. He has no life."

Kiki snorted. "There you go again, volunteering your brother for stuff he has no say in."

Trace shrugged. "Well, he *doesn't* have a life."

"He's got two kids!"

Trace suddenly looked at his watch. "Speaking of kids, we'd better go get working on having some of our own," he said, a mischievous grin on his face. "Ready to retire for the evening, Mrs. Rocklin?"

Kiki laughed and climbed off his lap. "Uh oh," she said. "Are you going to start that old song and dance again?"

He stood up from the chair, stretching his big body out. "I sure am," he said. "The melody, the harmony, and everything else."

Kiki continued to laugh as she put her hands over her ears. "We have three grown children between us," she reminded him yet again. The having-children conversation had been a running gag between them for the past month, only Trace was fairly serious about it. "Do we really want to start over with kids of our own? I'm not getting any younger, you know."

He whistled low for the dog, who left the fountain and trotted over in his direction. "Look," he said, pointing to the mutt. "All I have is Bullfrog. He's our only child and he's really ugly. I would like to have some better-looking children with you. You're only forty years old. I don't know why you think you're too old to have more children."

Kiki couldn't stop laughing. "Because I *am*."

He wouldn't let up. "Just one? Just one so I don't have to go the rest of my life giving all of my attention to that fat dog?"

She tried to push him away but he wouldn't budge. Trace swooped down and scooped her up into his muscular arms, carrying his giggling wife into the house as the dog followed, and continued up into their bedroom where he shut Stanley out for the night. For what he was about to do, he didn't want an audience. Undeterred, Stanley went to find his cozy-comfy bed in the kitchen as on the floor over his head, Kiki and Trace got in more practice on how to conceive a child.

It was practice that would come to fruition. Ten months and two days after their wedding day, Trace got his wish. After fifteen hours of labor, Kiki gave birth to a nine-pound baby boy. Trace wept when the doctor put the squirming infant into his arms and gazing into his son's red face, he called him by his name—*Austin*, after the man who'd built the house he was conceived in.

Agua de la Vida.

For Trace and Kiki, the old house and its old fountain had blessed them all because life, as they knew it, continued on with a new generation.

Austin Richard Rocklin, and his parents, had great lives ahead of them.